For Jenny and Boo,
with love x

CHAPTER ONE

"Write down three targets. Three things you want to achieve by the end of your time at Burton Upper Primary School, Hamster Class," said Miss Harper in her best *I'm issuing instructions now, so you'd better jolly-well listen* voice.

I sighed and stared at my blank piece of paper. What did I want to achieve in the last three weeks of school? I glanced around and saw everyone else merrily scribbling away. What could they possibly be writing? What did she even mean by "targets"? I caught

Stan's eye next to me as he triumphantly exhaled and swept his hand over his brow, like he was wiping away sweat. I guess Stan has goals? Probably about continuing to be super confident and super laid back: two things I admired about him and two things *I* could never be.

Then I felt Miss Harper looming over me – it was difficult to miss her thanks to her baby-pink cardigan covered in neon-yellow bobbles. If I didn't start writing soon, she'd ask me a question, and she *knew* I hated speaking in class – or, for that matter, speaking anywhere, to anyone, other than Stan, my sister and my dad. Using my excellent skills of teacher avoidance, I started to write. Although what I actually wrote was:

1. I'm writing to make it look like I'm writing. Writey writey writ...

Well, that bought me a bit of time: Miss Harper moved on, the threat diminished, and I rubbed out what I'd written. But I knew she'd be back, so I did actually need some "targets". In desperation, I looked around the room and saw Sharon's cage. There was just a mound of wood shavings where I knew she was curled up, hiding from the rest of us.

Lucky her! I knew just how she felt.

But she did give me an idea...

1. Look after the class hamster at home for one weekend.

It's fair to say that I might have been a little hamster-obsessed. I have always felt a strange connection to these tiny, furry animals and have spent so much time reading up about them that I'm quite an expert these days. They may not be the flashiest or most exotic of animals, but perhaps that's why I like them. I can't remember when I started asking Dad for one of my own, but I was no closer now than when my "Get Olly a Hamster" campaign started many moons ago, largely thanks to Dad's total and utter weirdness about hamsters. His range of excuses included the notion that he was "allergic" to hamsters, that they were responsible for the Black Death, and that given a whiff of opportunity these cute fluff-balls would tear out your jugular. When I tried to call him out on these very obvious lies, he just said, "I'm a scientist and I know these things." He had also pinned a "Top 10 Hamster-Related Injuries" sheet to our kitchen noticeboard that he *claimed* to have found on the internet, but, based on the terrible use of clip art, I think he made it up himself.

This year, as if just to rub it in, I was in Hamster Class. Now, *you* may think Hamster Class is a rubbish name, especially when compared to other class names. Granted, it's no Kingfisher Class or Starfish Class, but we were the only class able to have a class pet the same as our class name – ha! Take that, Wolf Class! *And* over the course of the year, Sharon had been taken home by almost everyone in Hamster Class. Everyone, that was, except me, because, of course, Dad just wouldn't hear of it.

It was a tragedy, but I did what I could for Sharon in the classroom. I spent a lot of time just sitting by her, and everyone had come to accept that while I may never speak aloud willingly, I *was* willing to leave a sheet of paper with grooming tips, lists of recommended foods, emergency advice and contact numbers next to her cage for everyone to follow. So, I guess you could say I was the unofficial classroom hamster monitor.

While I was wrapped up in my hamster thoughts, and still congratulating myself for thinking of my first target, Miss Harper's voice cut through the classroom again.

"You may be in your last ever month of primary school, but that's NO REASON to take your feet off the pedals. Plenty can be done in these three remaining weeks. Be *ambitious* with your targets! July might have started, but that does NOT mean you're already on holiday!"

Our Year 6 teacher was a mixture of strict scariness and quirky creativity, like a shark in sheep's clothing – almost literally. She definitely has a thing about wool, at least. At the start of the year, Miss Harper – who made all her alarmingly colourful cardigans herself – taught us all how to crochet a hamster, and now most of my classmates were on at least hamster number three. (Stan, to everyone's surprise, was a crochet wizard and had made at least eight!) We crocheted whenever we had spare time or while listening to the class reader. Finished ones were proudly displayed on the back wall of the classroom, but my own disastrous attempt – my hamster of shame – was skulking, unfinished, in a box in the corner. Some not-at-all-witty person (I assumed it was Horrendous Hugh) had drawn a large skull and crossbones on the box, with DANGER written across it.

I was still thinking about my failure of a crocheted hamster when:

"I said THREE targets, Olly!"

Miss Harper boomed, suddenly back at my desk. I quickly noted:

2. I want to finish my crochet hamster.

"Hmmm," Miss Harper said, eyeing my paper. "Maybe your third target could be something NOT related to hamsters? Just think what your dad achieved in his last term in Year 6."

That was SO TYPICAL of the teachers at this school. Just because my dad was a bit of a legend around here, there was this expectation that I must be secretly brilliant.

Well, it must be *very* secretly, because *I* haven't seen any sign of it.

The more this has been suggested over the years, the less brilliant I've felt. Me and Dad might look alike – Stan cracked up when he first saw an old photo of Dad, saying

Dad and I could be twins, with the same unmanageable, bouncy hair and oversized teeth – but I had always felt that Dad and me were NOTHING alike. Dad had been the space-prodigy-whizz-kid whose Year 6 science project from waaaaay back in the 1990s was still hanging from the ceiling in the school hall, gathering dust and cobwebs. And now, as Chief Scientific Officer of the local observatory, he regularly got invited to school to give space-themed talks and was treated like a rockstar by the teachers. To this day, next to the Head's office, framed in gold, hung Dad's final school report – kept on display to inspire us, apparently, because it was the most glowing report ever written. *My* reports were full of "Olly needs to have more confidence in his abilities if he is ever going to achieve anything", or "Olly's refusal to speak in class means I have no idea whether he has learnt anything this year", or "Olly who?" (That last one was in Year 4 – a particularly low point.) It seemed highly unlikely that, in the final weeks of school, I would suddenly develop a genius-level ability in ANYTHING.

Chances were that I'd leave school without actually having made any kind of impression at all. In that moment, I hurriedly wrote my third target:

3. I need to speak up and make an impact.

It was basically something written down on the spur of the moment. Something, really, to get Miss Harper off my back. It was definitely not something that I ever planned to do anything about.

***

I spent break time with Sharon, enjoying the peace of an empty classroom. I gingerly picked her out of her cage, gently stroking her fluffy fur and tickling her belly, but, as always, she continued to sleep. I considered that a compliment, that she had grown so comfortable with me handling her and giving her so much care and attention.

At least Sharon was safe now, having survived the weekend in the clutches of

Seren Simons, AKA the Doll Destroyer, known throughout the whole school for the terrifying doll heads she ties to her rucksack! I would probably never build up the courage to speak to Miss Harper about the LOTTERY that is picking a child at random to look after Sharon for weekends and holidays. Surely there needed to be an application form? At the very least, there should have been a ten-minute practical hamster-care presentation, followed by a written test!

But of course I wouldn't dare mention this to anyone – even Stan, because I couldn't quite trust him not to blurt it out. If he did, there was a risk I would actually have to *do* the presentation. And however much I was concerned for Sharon's welfare, it wasn't enough to get me to speak in public.

At the end of the day, while all the other kids waited for the bus, I watched as Dad pulled up in his embarrassingly boxy blue Toyota Cloud. ("This car's been rated top for safety five years running – can't ask for more than that!") Why couldn't he just let me get the bus with everyone else?

"Right, we just need to call in at Asda," he said. "We need nappies for Martha, not to mention her cookies, and I've got a hankering after some delicious, fresh pastries – what do you say?"

I groaned inwardly as I knew exactly what was coming. Dad had got it into his head that one way of "bringing me out of my shell" was to *force* me into massively awkward conversations with strangers. Force is too strong a word, actually, as I

know Dad only meant well. *Encouraged.*
That's a better word for it. *Cajoled.* He was
always coming up with reasons why I would
have to talk to shop assistants.

We arrived at the supermarket and,
lo and behold, Dad went off to get nappies
and cookies, leaving me to ask at the bakery
for the pastries that *Dad* wanted. I tried my
hardest to make my request at the counter,
avoiding eye contact, but my heart started
beating wildly and my mouth felt full of
sand and my mind went totally blank, and
the next thing I knew, a member of the
security team was being called over and an
announcement was being made about a "lost
and scared little boy"!

I was still cringing about the events at
the supermarket as I lay in bed that night.
My pastry failure highlighted the fact that
I would NEVER achieve the third target at

school and start speaking up. But maybe, just maybe, I could achieve the first target? If I did – somehow – convince Dad that I could look after Sharon for a weekend, he would see that I deserved to have a pet hamster *of my own*.

I allowed myself to imagine having a large cage beside my bed, full of soft bedding, tunnelling materials, a hamster wheel, nutritionally varied food and fresh water (everything listed on my Hamster Information Sheet next to Sharon, of course). As I drifted off, just at the edge of consciousness, I heard a *boing* noise, followed by a big splash. But it was not quite enough to disturb my fantasy and, as I slept that night, I was convinced I could actually hear the pittery-pattering sound of hamsters.

From Tibbles, Mission Lead for the Faithful on Operation O

To Fluffy the 1000th, the Great and Most Fluffisome, Tender-Hearted Leader of Hamsters

Date HCT 172,467

Most Tender-Hearted Leader,

We have arrived safely on the planet the Ancient Ones called Earth. Our journey from the Mothership was brief, but it was not without difficulties. I believe we are in the correct location, as pin-pointed by our researchers from the sacred stories passed down to us. However, the point of impact was much more ... *bouncy* than anticipated. We were deflected from our planned site and crashed into a nearby body of water.

Do not be concerned for us, great master! I am pleased to report that all in the landing party are alive and well. However, the spaceship is now submerged underwater and we are working on a plan to retrieve it.

Worry not; we are still focused on our mission of locating the wondrous O! We are all so excited to be in His presence, He who protected our Ancient Ones. Our faith in Him will surely soon be rewarded. We thank you, kind leader, for this historic opportunity. As promised, we will keep a low profile as we find out more about the divine O. He is close – I can sense it.

Your servant,

Tibbles

CHAPTER TWO

The next morning, I was about to head down for breakfast when I saw something that would stop anyone in their tracks. Downstairs, leaning on the breakfast bar, holding forth with a monotone voice that sounded as if it came more from his nose than his mouth, was our neighbour Mr Potter, the ceiling light reflecting off his shiny head. Dad always said we should feel sorry for him because he was clearly lonely. What I think Dad meant was that he was clearly a countdown short of a rocket launch. Mr

Potter is a science fiction fanatic, and ever since he found out that Dad works at the National Space Observatory, he's always coming round to ours with his latest, not-very-scientific space observations. Late last November, he had woken us up in the middle of the night, ranting about a "strange aura" hanging over the village, convinced that aliens had landed. Dad was not impressed to be dragged on a midnight walk with two sleepy children, only to discover that the Carters at 67 Barclay Lane had gone a bit over the top with their Christmas lights. So I was surprised Dad had even let Mr Potter in the house at seven a.m. on a weekday. As silently as possible, I opened Martha's safety gate but stayed put at the top of the stairs – I hoped Dad could get rid of Mr Potter quickly.

"Last night was a corker, Ozzy," Mr

Potter was saying. "I wouldn't be surprised if your detectors and what-nots in your super-duper science facility were all lit up like Christmas, with all the strange activity going on. My scanner picked up one, if not two, unidentified objects. I think it's really happening this time."

"Hold your jet-packs there, Mr Potter," soothed Dad. "The observatory's devices search the skies for all manner of things at all times. I would have been notified if something new had appeared. Let me tell you, especially regarding objects in close proximity to Earth, there's *never* anything new to get excited about. Your old scanners might be malfunctioning. It could have been a large bird! Or perhaps simply an unregistered spy satellite. Nothing interesting."

Unregistered spy satellites sounded pretty interesting to me, to be honest, and

I made the mistake of stepping on to the creaky staircase. Dad and Mr Potter looked up, and I cursed the open-plan design of our downstairs. There was no escape now.

"Ah, Olly," said Dad. "There you are. Why don't you tell Mr Potter what I'm always saying about alien life-forms?"

Argh. Why couldn't Dad just allow me to stay in the background? If I wanted to speak to adults, I would. I stared blankly at my feet, mentally willing Dad to understand that this was not going to happen. Awkward silence. My hand gripped the banister tightly. Was Dad really forcing me to do this? Especially after yesterday's supermarket failure! The silence was broken only by the rumbling from my tummy – was that fear or hunger? I started to worry that at this rate I may not get my Crunchy Golden Nobbles before I would have to leave for school.

Dad finally got the message, cleared his throat and said, "With our unparalleled technology, we are more convinced than ever that aliens do not exist, or contact would have been made by now. So there is no reason to worry about aliens posing a threat. The greatest threat to this planet is, quite simply, from humans ourselves."

"Pah! I should have known that's what you'd say. I bet there's someone in power that doesn't want us discovering the truth, so that's why all your *so-called* data is always so clean. And it's exactly the kind of thing we'll be discussing here," countered Mr Potter, puffing his chest out, and proudly tapping a faded T-shirt with what used to read "Alien Con XVII" on it (but now reads "A ... Con X") and a half-peeled alien face that now just looked like an egg. "See this? The next big convention is just over a week away!

I'll be there. And I won't be alone. WE'RE not alone. Aliens are out there. You can't keep denying it, Ozzy. I knew I was right to dig that pond. It's attracting them, like a giant signal, reflecting back to alien life-forms. Eighty-seven per cent of all UFO sightings take place near residences with a pond. What do you say about that?"

"Coincidence?" said Dad. "People really like ponds? Trust me, Mr Potter, there was a time when I hoped with all my heart to find aliens, but they simply are not out there." They'd had this conversation so many times, I was surprised Dad let Mr Potter into the house any more. But then

Dad changed his tone. "Everyone is entitled to their own beliefs. And, of course, I have the utmost respect for yours. Who knows, one day YOU might be proved right. But I'm glad you mentioned your pond. I was wondering if you'd given any more thought to getting rid of it? With Martha being on the move, I do worry that having such a big body of water close to our home is an unnecessary danger."

I rolled my eyes. Dad and his over-protectiveness! At least I now knew WHY Dad was willing to humour Mr Potter and listen to his wild tales. Aliens in his pond? As if! But that was still more likely than Martha falling into it. Martha, who was still completely baffled by her safety gate, would have to burst through a two-metre-high hedge to get to that pond.

"I'd be ever so grateful, Mr Potter,"

Dad pressed on. "I can't afford to replace the hedge with fencing, and you know how kids are; Martha might just crawl through. Please consider draining it."

"Yes, well, hmmm," said Mr Potter, suddenly keen to leave. "I'll leave you to your morning."

I almost felt sorry for him as he scurried out the back door, muttering to himself. But at least the coast was now clear for me to get to my Crunchy Golden Nobbles!

> Chatroom for Alien Contact

WeAreNotAlone65: Did anyone else pick up unusual activity last night – July 3 – at around 22:15? In the Malcott area? I tried to quiz my contact at the Observatory about it, but he refused to engage. I trust my scanner and I KNOW it's logged something new. Something exciting. Something close by! Just because I'm not a space "expert" or a science "professional", it doesn't make my observations – and potential discoveries – any less relevant.

AlienCat: Well said! Nothing picked up here, but I believe you xx

1234Chaos: Just because THE OFFICIAL story is it didn't happen, doesn't mean it didn't, bruv

PartKlingon99: Hello, fellow believer! Are you also using the model TX375 Scanner from the 1990s? Best scanner ever! I don't know why the government ever

CHAPTER THREE

Dad dropped me at school as normal. It was only three kilometres which, thanks to my research, I knew to be far less distance than the average hamster scampers in a night. Not that I wanted to be allowed to run to and from school! The daily car rides I didn't mind so much, but I did wish Dad would stop walking me those final few metres into school and kissing me goodbye. It wasn't a great look for an eleven-year-old.

I could see Stan's lanky shape as he loitered in the school corridor, waiting for me. He waved at Dad, who called, "Have a good day!" Stan gave a dramatic bow, which, for anyone else doing it, would be weird in the extreme, but over the last two terms I'd become used to Stan's particular style.

Ah, Stan! My one friend. I met Stan on his first day at Burton Upper Primary School at the start of Year 6. If anyone else would have bothered to get to know him, they'd have realized how ace he is. Oh, he's friendly to everyone, but he is how he is and doesn't pretend otherwise. Unfortunately for Stan that means always saying EXACTLY the wrong thing at the wrong time. Or maybe that should be the wrong thing at the right time? The right thing at the wrong time? Whatever. You get my meaning.

Let me give you an example. If you're a new kid in a small school, you are the star attraction for at least a week, when everyone jostles to befriend you. Often, the teacher will allocate a classmate to take care of you and "show you the ropes". Well, the only ropes at our school were the ones dangling from the gym equipment in the hall, which Amelia Fletcher would climb halfway up and then get stuck and cry. EVERY. SINGLE. GYM. LESSON. In Stan's case, his assigned classmate was Hugh. Of course Hugh was chosen. Hugh basically went through life as "the chosen one". Perhaps it was something to do with his halo of pale hair, sparkling smile and impressive athletic abilities. Pupils and teachers alike treated Hugh as a god. But, then again, it could have been because of the free sweets he was always giving out.

The first thing Hugh said to Stan was, "Do you know Botham Buys Best in the village?"

To which Stan responded, "Yes, my mum went in there at the weekend and couldn't believe how much everything cost. Botham Buys Best? Botham Buys Rubbish And Sells It At Massively Inflated Prices, more like. Mum said it's daylight robbery."

Now, if Stan had just waited a split second before jumping in with this nugget from his mum, he might have stopped to consider *why* Hugh was asking that question and possibly also thought back to the moment, just a few seconds before, when Miss Harper said, "Hugh Botham – you will be making Stan feel welcome and showing him the ropes."

So, yes, Stan managed, with his very first words at Burton Upper Primary School, to insult the most popular kid in class: Hugh Botham. Son of the owner of Botham Buys Best, the Burton village shop. Miss

Harper, who was very keen on the "fizzy ferret" chews Hugh brought in, reassigned responsibility for Stan to me and the rest, as they say, is history.

From the start, I appreciated Stan's bluntness. His first words to me were: "Why are you showing me these filthy ropes that smell of feet?" In that moment, I knew we'd be great friends, because I had been wondering exactly the same thing but hadn't been brave enough to question Miss Harper's instructions.

So, for the whole of Year 6, it had been me and Stan on one side, and Hugh and his cronies on the other – but this had been a marked improvement on Years 3, 4 and 5, when it was me on my own versus the Hugh Botham Fan Club. (The club did actually exist, I heard Seren Simons whispering about it one break time.) Between Stan's arrival and becoming the unofficial hamster monitor, Year 6 had been my best year so far – and it was about to come to an end.

The school day started, as always, with us crocheting while Miss Harper took the register. Stan and I sat together at the front, which sometimes helped me forget there was a whole class behind me who didn't like us – something that didn't seem to bother Stan.

"Today we are going to—" Miss Harper started to announce, closing the register, but she stopped mid-sentence. "Stanley Crump! What on earth are you doing? That looks nothing like a hamster!"

I was so focused on unknotting yet another mistake in my own Frankenhamster that I hadn't even noticed what Stan had been doing. For some reason, he was crocheting with red wool.

"Oh, you know, Miss," said Stan, "I've

crocheted so many hamsters now that I'm a bit bored of them, so I'm trying to work out how to crochet something new. It's – erm – a surprise."

For once, Stan looked sheepish. He glanced to the back of the room – no idea why – to where Amelia Fletcher and Seren Simons sat, probably whispering about how awesome Hugh is.

Miss Harper appeared to decide that there was no point in arguing. "Well," she said, "I look forward to seeing what you come up with."

"Thanks, Miss!" said Stan with a little wink. Stan may always be putting his foot in his mouth with kids our age, but his level of cheekiness with grown-ups was something I could only observe and admire. Teachers loved him; it was something about his buoyant confidence. "You were saying, Miss ... today we're going to...?"

"Oh, that's right. We need to plan our Hamster Class Leavers' Party on the last day of term, which is traditionally planned by two Year 6s: one taking the lead and another as second-in-command. This is a great honour for those pupils and always looks great on a school record. So, we need to think about who—"

"I nominate Hugh!" squealed Amelia.

There were grunts of approval and, turning around in my seat, I rolled my eyes as Hugh stood up and slowly spun with his arms aloft, his pale curls glinting like a crown on his head, accepting the adoration of the whole class (well, 28/30ths of the class, or 14/15ths, if you want to get clever about it – me and Stan were *not* joining in).

"I humbly accept this nomination," Hugh announced.

"I nominate Olly!" Stan suddenly shouted, loud enough for the whole school to hear.

I jumped in my seat.

WHAT? How could Stan—

Just then, in the midst of my shock, I sensed something moving out of the corner of my eye. A quick jolt of movement across the floor. *Sharon?!* Panicked, I peered under the table and all around, but there was nothing there. Strange. I looked over at her cage and there she was, her sleeping body wedged in the corner, fur poking slightly out of the bars. I was vaguely aware of the class laughing and of Miss Harper speaking, but I was certain I'd seen *something*.

"So is that a yes, Olly?" I heard Miss Harper ask.

"Erm, yes, Miss Harper?"

"Great, that's settled then. Hugh will be in charge of organizing the class's Leavers' Party with Olly helping. Perfect!"

Oh no! What had I agreed to? What had Stan done?

"*Erm, yes, Miss Harper?*" was four words – my average total of spoken words per half term, so I'd already used up my quota for the next three weeks – and now I was expected to help with the Leavers' Party. With Hugh? The walls of the classroom started to swim at the edges of my vision and a sicky taste had appeared in my mouth.

Stan nudged me with his shoulder and grinned, while Hugh was giving me an evil glare with icy-blue eyes that were perfectly designed for doing just that. Hugh hated Stan – although I'm not sure Stan even noticed – but he absolutely LOATHED me.

What kind of a friend would set me up to work with someone who, for years, had treated me worse than something you'd find on the bottom of your shoe? I grabbed Stan at break to ask him exactly that.

"I'm *trying* to help you," he said. "Remember your third target? Making an impact? I know you hate speaking up, but hear me out: being second-in-command is all behind the scenes! This way you'll achieve your target, have something that looks great on your school record, and I'm sure this will help you stop cowering from Hugh. You're a team now – he has to work with you! You never know, you could become friends!"

I was about to point out that the likelihood of me and Hugh becoming friends was roughly the same as aliens suddenly appearing in our village – when another movement caught my eye, a blur flashing past my toes and along the corridor.

From Tibbles, Mission Lead for the Faithful on Operation O

To Fluffy the 1000th, the Great and Most Fluffisome, Tender-Hearted Leader of Hamsters

Date HCT 172,468

Most Tender-Hearted Leader,

I write with glorious news! We have, indeed, located the divine and celestial O. He is just as described in the stories passed down by our Ancient Ones, unchanged since the time of the Great Departure. Our images of O are, indeed, so true to life that it's almost like he stepped off the pages of our picture books. We must congratulate our mural-painters, sculptors and miniaturists.

Imagine – in the lifetime of our colony, from its foundation by Fluffy the First and Scruffy the Splendid, right through to your reign, most tender-hearted leader – O has been a constant presence in the universe!

Our spaceship remains inaccessible, but we are working on solutions and I hope to report back with happy news soon. My fellow faithful are keeping their nocturnal habits, working at night to establish a base here, and gathering special mementos of O for us to bring back to the colony. We already have quite a stash of souvenirs that you will love and that we are excited to present to you as thanks for making this expedition happen.

In my role as Mission Lead, I have the honour of following O on his daily habits. It is my privilege to see His life and His routine, although I am determined to remain undetected, as directed. I am learning a great amount that was never mentioned in The Stories. For example, O lives with an old, huge and decrepit version of Himself, who He calls "Dad", and also shares His home with a tyrannical figure I have heard Him call "Martha". My communications device has failed to translate these words, so I can only guess at their meaning. "Dad" is perhaps human for "servant" and "Martha", I assume, means "one with uncontrollable rage" or "devourer of brown discs". Perhaps He has taken these sorry people in, thanks to His goodness?

If the translation mode is faulty, perhaps the communications device is also failing to send these messages. I wonder why I have not received word from you?

Your servant,
Tibbles

CHAPTER FOUR

You know when you sense someone looking at you and you look up and someone IS looking at you? For the remainder of Tuesday and the whole of Wednesday, it was like that. All. The. Time. And yet, whenever I looked up, either no one was paying me the least bit of attention (as always) or there was no one else around.

I tried to explain the feeling to Stan, who draped a long arm over my shoulder and simply said, "You're losing it, mate. Maybe I was wrong to volunteer you for the party. You're clearly not ready. My bad."

But the paranoid feeling had nothing to do with the party, and I was fairly convinced it didn't have anything to do with Hugh, however much he hated me.

And he *really* hated me.

***

Let me explain. Living in the tiny village of Malcott meant, from Year 3, kids started to attend Burton Upper Primary School in the neighbouring, larger village of Burton. On the very first day of Year 3, as we all sat on the carpet, Mr Thomas asked for a volunteer to read the register. Twenty-nine eager little hands immediately reached for the sky. Every child was soon on their feet, jumping and wheezing, as if being picked to read the register was something their lives depended on.

Every child, that is, except me. Even when I was seven, reading the register was the stuff of nightmares. I knew I would turn bright red and stumble over words; I was not up to the task. So I sat there quietly. And that was my biggest mistake.

"You are sitting BEAUTIFULLY," exclaimed the teacher, pointing me out with a bony finger. "Everyone should take a lesson from Oliver Brown there. What lovely manners. The job is yours!"

NO!

By trying to be unnoticeable, somehow I had stood out. As I made my way past my new classmates, trying to avoid jutting knees and splayed fingers on the carpet, I could already feel my heart pound and my throat dry up. My palms were so sweaty, I could barely grasp the register, which was bigger than my head. I cleared my throat and started with the first name on the list.

"H... H... H... Hu... Hoo... Hmmm." This was even trickier than I thought it was going to be. I paused, took a deep breath and tried again. "Huge Bottom."

Mayhem.

The class erupted into hysterics.

Children were rolling on the floor, grasping their sides. There were howls. There were tears. There was foot stomping. Judging by the smell, at least one child wet themselves.

"MY NAME IS HUGH BOTHAM!" screeched a piercing voice. It belonged to a child with white-blond hair. And although his face had been as pale as his hair moments before, it was now bright red.

How was I to know that THAT was how you pronounce the name "Hugh"? I'd never even heard that name before, let alone seen it written down. And mispronouncing the name Botham was an easy mistake.

The next day, following Mr Botham's visit to the Head, Mrs Scout, the whole class got a lecture on how anyone EVER caught calling Hugh Botham "Huge Bottom" would get detention for a month and their family would be banned from the village corner shop, Botham Buys Best, for all time. This announcement was followed by the handing out of packets of sweets from the shop to everyone in class.

Except for me.

From then on, you were either "Team Hugh" or you were Olly. And I don't mean "Team Olly". Just me, alone.

***

Now, thanks to Stan, Hugh and I would be stuck working together. But I was far more distracted and disturbed by the weird pittery-pattery sounds that I could hear when I lay awake at night. This was exactly the kind of thing NOT to mention to my dad, or I'd be straight down to A&E for a brain scan or something. (Unless a limb is actually falling off, I have learned that with Dad it's best keeping scrapes and symptoms to myself.) And I was fairly sure what I was hearing wasn't *in* my head but somewhere *out there*.

SENSING things was bad enough, but then I began to notice things going missing. Nothing much, but enough to be annoying. It started when I couldn't find my best rubber that I always keep on my desk at home. You know the kind – that rare rubber that actually rubs out without smudging? My suspicion was that Martha had nabbed it – she was always going into my room without permission. And what would she want with a decent rubber at the age of two? She is only interested in it because it's shaped like a purple unicorn. I accused her, but she turned on the waterworks and did the whole "big sad eyes" thing at Dad and he took her side. *And* she got a cookie.

"Of course your sister wouldn't take

your belongings. Look at her. What an angel!" I'm sure Dad said, although I wasn't really listening because I had already known how the conversation would go.

Following the case of the missing rubber, I also lost (or misplaced, as Dad insisted) a pencil sharpener, a Pokémon sock, my Minecraft nail clippers and my Lego key ring. It was most disturbing and I continued to suspect that Martha was at the bottom of it. When I lost my favourite underpants, however, that was harder to pin on Martha as I could not think of a decent reason why she'd want my grotty old kecks. (In case you're interested, they're my favourite because they're covered in Os.) I turned my whole room upside down trying to find them. If it wasn't Martha taking these things, then who? And what could they possibly want with my stuff?

"You're just being paranoid," claimed Stan when I reeled off the list of missing items. "Get some sleep and you'll soon realize that this sense of heebie-jeebies is all in your head."

In his blunt way, Stan did have a point. I probably just needed rest. That night, I made a sleep mask from my remaining Pokémon sock and borrowed Dad's ear plugs. If I heard anything now, I'd know it was definitely in my head.

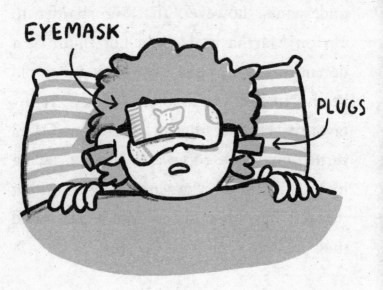

EYEMASK

PLUGS

From Tibbles, Mission Lead for the Faithful on Operation O

To Fluffy the 1000th, the Great and Most Fluffisome,
Tender-Hearted Leader of Hamsters

Date HCT 172,469

Most Tender-Hearted Leader,

I do hope you are receiving my communications. There is so much to report.

As I was on duty, watching O this evening, I realized He had cocooned Himself from the outside world, so I was safe to approach closer without fear of being seen. To be in the presence of such greatness was humbling indeed. As I watched Him sleep – the deep sleep of the truly blessed – I reminded myself of the tales of His goodness. Of the Great Wheel of Joy. Of the Miracles of Endless Water and Food.

At that moment, my mind was filled with all the questions I have wanted to ask Him over the years. Those questions only He could answer, such as: "Why did He make it so our cheek pouches could get so big – exactly what did He want us to keep in there?"

Earth is a confusing and complex place. The objects we are saving for our return seem to throw up more questions than they answer: what is the significance of the small purple creature with a tail that appears to have been ... rubbed away? Why does a tiny plastic man have a chain drilled into his head, which is attached to a shiny loop? Is this some kind of unusual punishment on this planet? Does the loop represent the wondrous O? I am hopeful that at least some of my questions will find answers here. I do, however, understand your warning to proceed with caution. We will not alert O to our presence.

I gave silent thanks in the darkness. And I'm not ashamed to admit that there, overwhelmed by the honour of being the first of our colony to be so close to Him, I did a poo. Or four.

Your servant,

Tibbles

ALIEN
CONSPIRACY
CHAT

> Chatroom for Alien Contact

WeAreNotAlone65: My scanner keeps registering a faint signal, emitted from the Malcott area. As far as I can tell, this is very close to my house! It started up a few days ago, just before my last post about the unusual activity. This has got my senses tingling. *Something* is close by. Something BIG. I can't help but feel that this is my destiny. Aliens *are* among us. And if I can prove that, I'll be famous! Who's excited?

Steven: You're talking tripe, mate

ScarySpice222: Click on this link for all your alien needs

PartKlingon99: I'm excited for you – but, take my word for it, this will be all hushed up, just like what happened to me on a bright and starless night way back in 2003. I obviously can't go into too many specifics, as you never know who might be on here, but safe to say I got more visitors than I expected on my birthday that year, at 121 Garven Road. I was just blowing out my candles when BOOM. A huge flash of light burst

CHAPTER FIVE

I hated to admit it, but Stan had probably been right about the sleep. I woke the next morning with the sun glinting through my curtains, and I felt much better. It's amazing how a proper rest can completely change your outlook. I even didn't mind about the chocolate chip cookie crumbs I found on my bedside table – *Martha*. I simply swept the four quite big crumbs into my hand and, when Martha wasn't looking, mixed them in with her Weetabix. I actually felt like a kind big brother for this. It was a nice feeling.

At school, when I admitted that his suggestion of a decent sleep had worked, Stan did a victory lap around the classroom, shouting "I was right!" while everyone else glared at him. I was fairly sure he'd continue the laps until the teacher came but, weirdly, he slid straight back into his chair as soon as Amelia walked in. Later that day, in my refreshed state, I managed not to mind Hugh's obvious hatred for me while he droned on about all his rubbish ideas for the Leavers' Party, which largely involved listing everything he was going to get his dad to donate from their shop. I even managed to mutter "It's a nut-free school" when Hugh included dry-roasted peanuts in his snack list. I'm not sure which of us was more surprised by my speaking – I jumped like someone behind me had done it, and Hugh just accepted my correction in stunned silence. It was during afternoon break that everything changed.

In my role as hamster monitor, I'd allocated Thursday afternoon breaks for hamster playtime. I can't say this was ever particularly successful, as Sharon slept through all my efforts to get her to interact. This break, I gently encouraged Sharon to get into the hamster ball I'd never actually seen her use. I was fairly certain she was only *pretending* to be asleep. All attempts failed so I gave up and started refilling her water bottle at the sink, and that's when I turned and saw it.

There, outside Sharon's cage, gazing at Sharon almost as if in a trance, was *another hamster*! The water bottle slipped out of my grasp without its lid on fully and its contents exploded over the floor, but I could not tear my eyes away from what I was seeing. The noise disturbed the new hamster and, as I ignored the feeling of Sharon's water seeping into my socks, I watched it react to me like a cartoon character in shock. Its eyes went huge like they were trying to squeeze out of their sockets. It screamed. It jumped. Its fur stuck out like it had been electrocuted. And then it ran back and forth behind Sharon's cage, as if looking for a place to hide.

Not knowing what to do, I said, "STOP!"

A tiny squeak emanated from it.

And then it stopped.

It looked at me. It tilted its head to one side. And then the other. And then – and I swear this actually happened – it rose on to its hind legs and kind of bowed to me. And again. And again. This was not like any behaviour I'd ever come across in my hamster research. What was going on?

Slowly, I stepped forwards and lowered my hands, to try to encourage it to come to me. I held my breath as it hesitated. There was something in its eyes that suggested it was working out what to do. Did hamsters think that deeply about their actions? I glanced over at Sharon, who was sleeping as always – she *never* seemed to be thinking deeply. But I was sure this hamster was. After a few seconds just waiting there, the hamster gave a little shake, pattered forwards, touched my outstretched fingers with a tentative paw – and fainted.

Thankfully, I could see the new hamster's little ribs moving as it breathed, so I knew it was still alive. I would have felt horrible if I had shocked a hamster *to death* – what kind of hamster monitor would I have been then? While this new hamster was spark-out, lying on the counter beside Sharon's cage, I was able to examine it. Unlike Sharon's shaggy fluff, which was largely white and dotted with a smattering of browns and beige, this hamster's fur was sleek and golden. And its body was much smaller. I know enough about hamsters to know this wasn't a baby. I'd say it was a dwarf hamster, rather than a Syrian one like Sharon. The size of the hamster wasn't its most unusual feature, however, as wrapped around its middle was a tiny, circular black box! Where on earth had this strange hamster come from?

As I was asking myself this question, it opened its eyes. I said, in my softest voice, "Hello, you. Where did you come from?" and gave it a very light stroke over its head.

A slight squeaking came from the black box, followed by a clicking sound from the hamster itself. It was louder than any noise I'd ever heard Sharon make,

even at her most delighted (generally when eating blueberries I'd smuggled in from home). Then it did a little puddle of wee. And fainted. Again.

With break about to end and an unconscious strange hamster in the classroom, I had to think quickly. I wondered about burying it in amongst the crocheted hamsters, but there was a risk that the hamster might escape, and I needed to keep this little guy safe. If it was someone's pet, they certainly weren't doing a great job of looking after it. Maybe the thing around its middle was a clue to its owner, like a dog ID tag? Then there was all the fainting to look into, which I was sure was not normal hamster behaviour. At that moment, I made up my mind: I was going to take this hamster home. I just needed to get through the last lesson of the day, and there was only one safe place for my new friend: my class drawer. I had just managed to place it in there, along with a small paint palette of water and a handful of Sharon's food, when my classmates filed back in.

I could barely concentrate during the lesson, distracted by the joyous prospect of looking after my very own hamster! But I'd have to keep it hidden from everyone, especially Dad. In hindsight, I probably shouldn't have put blueberries in there because, as soon as the lesson started, I could hear some clicking coming from the drawer. I was relieved that the hamster had regained consciousness, but now I had a different problem: what to do about the noise?

While the rest of us crocheted – or, in my case, knotted wool entirely at random – Miss Harper asked Hugh to present his (or, I suppose, ours – but definitely his) ideas about the School Leavers' Party. Even though Hugh normally seemed so confident, he actually appeared to be struggling at the front of the class as he spoke, which should have given me a *little* pleasure – it was Hugh after all – but I imagined myself in his position, standing up at the front, and even the thought of it made my palms sweat. But his stilted presentation was not enough to cover the growing noise from my drawer – CLICK. CLICK. CLICK – and I had to act. I went to rub my sweaty hands together and inadvertently gave a little clap. That was it!

Clapping!

My first claps were just tentative taps, done with my eyes squeezed shut, as if bracing myself for something bad to happen. Nothing bad did happen, so I allowed one eye to squint open. My pitiful tapping wasn't doing a good enough job of covering the hamster noise. I needed to be braver. I swallowed hard, gathering strength from the thought of my poor, scared tiny hamster, and forced myself to clap with more gusto. I was soon giving a one-person round of applause.

Hugh looked a little surprised, but he seemed to accept that this was part of my job as second-in-command. As Hugh tried to explain his idea for the party finale, which would involve him standing onstage, wearing a crown, and throwing packets of

Haribo at his adoring fans, my clapping became whooping and then the whooping became stomping. By the end of the lesson, everyone was feeling very enthusiastic about the party. Only Stan was looking rather confused by my sudden transformation into Hugh's chief cheerleader.

At the end of the day, when Miss Harper led the class out to the playground, I stayed behind, pretending to check on something for Sharon. As soon as the last class member was out the door, I grabbed my lunch box and stabbed several holes in it with a pair of compasses from Miss Harper's desk. Then I part-filled the box with some more of Sharon's food and some of her spare bedding, before carefully opening my drawer. There, quivering slightly in the darkest corner, on what was now a quite soggy set of instructions on hamster care, was the mysterious new hamster. I placed it in the box and, hoping that I wasn't about to traumatize it for life, pushed the box into my bag.

I whispered, "Don't worry, little one. I'll look after you from now on."

From Tibbles, Mission Lead for the Faithful on Operation O

To Fluffy the 1000th, the Great and Most Fluffisome, Tender-Hearted Leader of Hamsters

Date HCT 172,470

Most Tender-Hearted Leader,

I have disgraced myself. I was blinded for one moment by a hamster unlike any I'd ever seen. Her fluff! Her size! Truly, she is a vision, possibly sent by O Himself. In this moment of infatuation, like being struck with lightning, I let my guard down and alerted O to my presence. I have failed in the one mission you had entrusted to me.

The wondrous O spoke to me, allowing my communications device to start up properly for the first time. It translated the glorious O's words as "potatoes" – which was so surprising it stopped me in my tracks. And then He said, "Mountain jam. Where did blossom tickle?" This was not quite the great wisdom The Stories led us to believe O was known for. This surely proves my communications device *is* faulty.

Thanks to His goodness and mercy, I am now under His care. It is perhaps a SIGN that our only way to return to our colony is with His help. My fellow faithful are struggling with plans to retrieve our spaceship and I worry what the water will be doing to the mechanisms the longer it sits submerged. Surely the wondrous O will reward our continued faith in Him and help us? My failure to remain undetected has perhaps provided an opportunity to secure our safe return. I await a message from you, most tender-hearted leader, and I sincerely hope that you are not angry at this turn of events.

Your servant,

Tibbles

P.S. I am excited to report that food given to me by O is unlike anything we have ever consumed on our planet. The taste and textures of the sustenance given to me by His hand is beyond compare. Truly, it is the nectar of the gods. I hope to bring much of it back on our return journey, so all in our colony can feast and rejoice in Him.

From Fluffy the 1000th, the Great and Most Fluffisome,
Tender-Hearted Leader of Hamsters
To Tibbles, Servant
Date HCT 172,472

Servant,

Well, it seems like this is the only solution, doesn't it? The success of the mission depends on the spaceship, so it needs to be retrieved at all costs. I have tried controlling the ship remotely but that doesn't appear to work either. Landing in water really stuffed our plans. As you have made your presence known to O, you might as well seek his assistance in getting the spaceship out and operational. Only then can this mission be completed.

F

CHAPTER SIX

That evening, my main worry was how to keep the hamster a secret at home. I hurried through my tea, which did not go unnoticed, so it was followed by a lecture from Dad on the dangers of choking. Thankfully, I survived and escaped to my room.

Following its big adventure, the hamster seemed very tired. Not wanting to stress it further, I tried to keep as quiet as possible and decided to leave the strange black box around its middle for now – it didn't seem to be bothering it. Thankfully, the hamster had stopped fainting every time I touched it and it even managed to sit in the palm of my hand, where it fitted perfectly. We spent some happy time just sitting in silence.

I have to say, it gazed at me rather adoringly. Were those *tears* coming into its eyes?

I placed the hamster back in the lunch box, and I settled down to sleep with an enormous sense of satisfaction. A hamster had come into my life, and I wasn't about to question that. Unsurprisingly, I dreamt of hamsters. Lots of dream hamsters, swirling around my room.

Something woke me with a jolt – and I jumped up and switched on my night light.

There, in the dim light, were more hamsters! It wasn't a dream! All tiny, sleek and golden, all running, one after the other, around the floor by my bed in a circle!

I knew I was awake, but I still couldn't believe what I was seeing. I fumbled for my lunch box, and opened it, then sighed with relief that *my* hamster was still sleeping away. I nudged it awake, unable to tear my eyes from the weird running ring of hamsters.

When my hamster saw them, it jumped out of its box on to the bedside table and

started chattering away in a range of hisses, squeaks and chirps – noises I was used to from Sharon. But then I tuned into another kind of noise – a sound coming from the hamster's little black box.

"Tibbles. Tibbles. Tibbles," was what I heard. Whenever the hamster squeaked, its black box made this noise.

I had no idea what "Tibbles" meant, but I do know when a hamster is not happy. It was having a right go at the others! They stopped running and gathered together on my rug, making it look like it had suddenly grown golden, pulsating fur. There must have been at least thirty or forty of them. Where on earth had they come from?

And, even though I couldn't be a hundred per cent sure about this, why did it look like they were hanging their heads in shame?

My hamster's chattering was getting louder and louder. I feared it would wake Dad up.

"Hey!" I whispered as loudly as I dared.

Suddenly, all the hamsters' attention was on me. Perhaps you will never experience what it is like to have lots of hamsters staring at you, but it's not something you ever get used to – and it certainly wasn't something I was ready for then. As I hesitated, working out my next steps, the most curious thing happened: one by one they started *bowing* at me. It was strange enough when the first hamster did this at school, but a whole rug's worth of hamsters bowing in wave after wave was super weird!

"Stop!" I hissed, gesturing with my hands.

The hamsters copied what I was doing.

I ran my fingers through my hair in

confusion – and the hamsters copied my action again. What was going on?

"*Where* have you little guys come from?" I whispered, circling my hands around, palms open, in an action I hoped would signify "where".

The hamsters simply copied me, moving their paws in circles.

I threw my hands up in exasperation. And so did the hamsters. I knew pretty much everything an eleven-year-old could know about hamsters, but here I was, faced with a – what's the collective noun for hamsters? – a *horde* of hamsters, and I was incapable of making myself understood. I shrugged my shoulders – as did the hamsters.

Almost as if it sensed my frustration, my hamster started squeaking again from the bedside table, with the black box echoing along: "Tibbles, Tibbles, Tibbles."

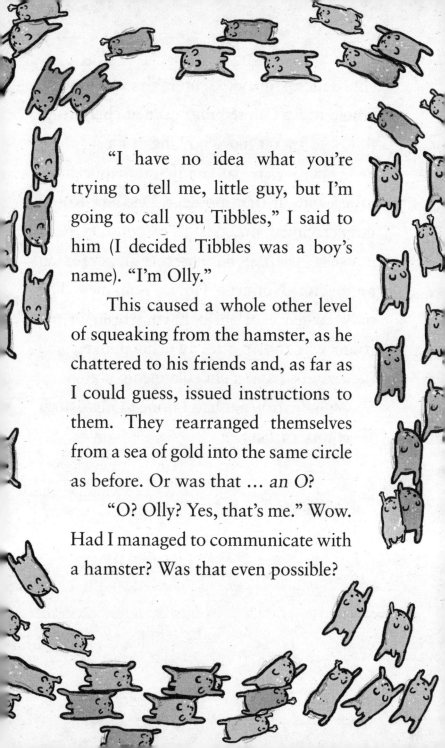

"I have no idea what you're trying to tell me, little guy, but I'm going to call you Tibbles," I said to him (I decided Tibbles was a boy's name). "I'm Olly."

This caused a whole other level of squeaking from the hamster, as he chattered to his friends and, as far as I could guess, issued instructions to them. They rearranged themselves from a sea of gold into the same circle as before. Or was that … *an O?*

"O? Olly? Yes, that's me." Wow. Had I managed to communicate with a hamster? Was that even possible?

Tibbles squeaked something else and the whole room erupted into excited chattering, followed by yet more bowing at me.

There were so many more questions to ask but, at that moment, Dad's bedroom door creaked and, as if responding to a gunshot, all the hamsters disappeared in an instant. Not even Tibbles remained. The only evidence of them having been in my room was rather a lot of what looked like the crumbs from a chocolate chip coo—

Oh dear. What had I done to my sister's Weetabix earlier?

From Tibbles, Mission Lead for the Faithful on Operation O

To Fluffy the 1000th, the Great and Most Fluffisome, Tender-Hearted Leader of Hamsters

Date HCT 172,470

Most Tender-Hearted Leader,

A response! I am so relieved. I feared that we would be lost to the colony for ever!

Thank you, dear leader, for agreeing to my plan to ask the wondrous O for His help with the ship. I hadn't realized the spaceship could be controlled remotely, either, although perhaps the ship has sustained too much damage in the water.

More has happened here, and many of the Faithful have now been seen by the divine O. Unfortunately, due to my faulty device, we are yet to communicate in any meaningful way, but I believe He is happy with our presence. He continues to speak in undecipherable riddles, although he has acknowledged my name, which I see as progress.

If I could communicate properly, I would, of course, prioritize asking Him about the spaceship, but there is so much more I wish to discuss with Him, especially about my observations on the planet of our origins. Even from a brief time on Earth, I see that there was much our Ancient Ones did not tell us, or much that they themselves did not understand. The planet is absolutely crawling with humans. Some appear to be large, slow and wrinkled, while others are small and loud. They only seem to use two of their four legs for moving around. This way of walking was, of course, reported in The Stories of the Ancient Ones, but it is funny to see in real life. Why would He design us with our amazing ability to run at super speed, both forwards and backwards, yet give Himself a mode of moving around that is slow and cumbersome? His wisdom is not for me to question, of course!

In our stories, the Car was a dangerous creature, gobbling up humans and spewing out smoke. But this is not the case, at least not now - there are many Cars, and humans actually LIKE these beasts! They enter into them voluntarily! Perhaps, in the time we have been away, the humans have tamed them? I will stay vigilant for the divine O's sake, in case these Cars are playing a terrible trick.

I hope you see that our mission is still proceeding with every chance of success. And now, if we prove ourselves to be His dedicated and loyal followers, surely our request - our prayer - for help with our spaceship will be met with sympathy and

action. I just need to work out how to make
myself understood.

Your servant,

Tibbles

CHAPTER SEVEN

The next morning, I got up super early. Instead of gobbling down my usual bowl of Crunchy Golden Nobbles, I searched for evidence of the hamsters around the house ... but I couldn't find any. Not even a single poo. And Tibbles had disappeared with the rest of them.

In the cold light of day, it all seemed too impossible to be true. I couldn't have just imagined all those hamsters, could I? Dad was unimpressed that I'd "forgotten" my lunch box at school: my holey lunch box was pushed under my bed – the only proof that the previous night had happened. As Dad prepared my lunch (into an old ice-cream tub), Martha squealed in frustration at her online "Toddler Tippy-Toes" dance programme. Wherever I put myself, while trying not to make it obvious I was on the hunt for quite a few hamsters, I just got in Martha's way. Eventually, Dad, in the interest of keeping Martha happy, suggested unlocking the netting around my trampoline so I could have a jump – after he'd performed his twenty-five-point trampoline safety check, of course. I prepared myself for a long wait, but Dad suddenly shouted to me from the bottom of the garden. I ran out to him.

"Look at this, Olly. Look!"

It was obvious that something fairly major had happened to my trampoline. The side netting was torn open, and there was a big scorch mark on the trampoline itself.

"What do you think could have caused this?" he asked.

How was I supposed to know? He was supposed to be the clever one.

Dad tried to answer his own question: "Maybe it was a lightning strike, although I can't remember a storm. Or maybe there are village vandals going around." He paused and chortled. "Best not mention it to Mr Potter, eh? He'll see it as evidence of aliens invading, won't he?"

I laughed nervously at Dad's comment. But a thought had struck me. Although I couldn't work out remotely *how* this could have happened, wasn't it odd that my trampoline had been trashed around the same time that a load of very strange hamsters had appeared? Could the two be related? I thought about this as I watched

Dad dismantle the trampoline's netting, propping parts up against his shed. All I wanted to do was get to school and tell Stan about everything that had happened. Thankfully, Dad realized the time and finally bundled me and Martha into the car, ready for the school run.

**

It is fair to say, Stan was rather dubious about my story.

"So, you found a hamster at school, took it home and then you woke up to find lots of hamsters in your room?"

"Yes."

"Bowing hamsters?"

"Yes."

"And you think these same hamsters trashed your trampoline?"

"Er, maybe?"

"Were you recently hit on the head?"

"No."

"Did you recently eat something past its sell-by date?"

"No."

"Do you feel stressed out by the School Leavers' Party?"

"I don't think so. Are these questions relevant?"

"I'm just trying to gauge your state of mind. You do realize that what you have described cannot possibly have happened. Not that I'm accusing you of lying or anything."

Yet it felt very much like Stan was accusing me of lying. To be fair, I would probably have reacted the same if anyone had told me the same thing – although I would have been too, well … Olly to actually say anything about it.

With no actual proof, and a suspicion sneaking into my brain that I had *actually* imagined the whole thing, I let it go. After all, it was Friday so, of course, I had to spend my breaks preparing Sharon for her weekend away. Theo Redfern was taking her this weekend. It would be his second time with Sharon (and, if my memory serves me correctly, he did *not* do a good job keeping her water fresh last time). My mind flipped back to the sea of hamsters that had appeared in my room the previous night. I hoped it wasn't just a dream.

At the end of the day, while dealing with the handover of Sharon, I opened my drawer to take out an information sheet for Theo. There, to my surprise, was Tibbles! I gave a squeal of delight that I tried to change into a cough, and, before Tibbles could finish his bow to me, I slid my drawer shut again. Theo looked quite surprised not to have to read all my guidance on hamster care. I say surprised. Probably more relieved – but I had other things to worry about. As soon as Theo and Sharon were out the door, I plucked Tibbles from my drawer and felt a wave of happiness sweep over me. This was it – I was finally going to spend a *weekend* with a hamster! OK, so it wasn't Sharon – but perhaps Tibbles was even better. Sharon had never bowed to me. While Tibbles bowed repeatedly at me from my desk, I made holes in the lid of the ice-cream tub. It was only when Tibbles was safely stashed in my bag and I saw Dad that I realized I was doing something completely against Dad's wishes. I'd been so wrapped up in excitement the day before, when I first met Tibbles, this thought hadn't even dawned on me. But it was hammering in my brain now.

The car journey was agony. It wasn't Martha chuntering about "Stinky Olly" while kicking the back of my seat. It was Dad chatting away merrily about his day at the Observatory. A sack of bricks felt to settle in my stomach and all the saliva in my mouth disappeared.

I wasn't used to keeping secrets from Dad.

When he started asking if I'd remembered my lunch box, my tongue felt like a strip of sandpaper, but I managed to rasp that I had *no idea* where it was.

Great – now I was outright lying!

Of course, I knew exactly where my lunch box was. My actual lunch box was still under my bed, and my replacement ice-cream tub was stashed at the bottom of my school bag with Tibbles inside. Suddenly, I was paranoid that Dad would somehow *sense* a hamster nearby. And why was Martha going on about "Stinky Olly"? Could she *smell* something? I began to panic that I'd drop my bag so the ice-cream tub and Tibbles would fall out. Or that we'd be stopped by the police, who'd ask to check my bag. Or that I'd suddenly blurt out "hamsters!"

It's safe to say I was not coping well with my growing web of secrets and lies.

***

That night, having made my excuses and escaped to my bedroom for an early night, I struggled to sleep. Tibbles was back beside my bed, in my lunch box, and half of me hoped and prayed for the rest of the hamsters to return during the night. The other half of me kept thinking about Dad and his weirdness about hamsters. I just had to keep it all secret from Dad. That was all. Easy. I had no idea how he'd respond to seeing just Tibbles, let alone thirty or forty hamsters. Thankfully, at least, Dad's supposed "allergy" to hamsters seemed to have been a lie, as I suspected all along. As silence fell in the house and snoring started up from Dad's room, the pattering of tiny feet told me I was no longer alone.

I switched on my night light – they were back!

And this time, there were even *more* hamsters! They were on every single surface in my room, some lining up on my shelves and a few even hanging from my lampshade!

Tibbles, suddenly awake, started chattering instructions. After he'd finished squeaking, the hamsters formed an orderly queue at the foot of my bed, snaking around

my room and out on to the landing.

One by one, each hamster came forward, touched my foot and squeaked, clicked or, occasionally, fainted. (Tibbles seemed to have allocated four hamsters to roll away any unconscious ones, so as not to hold up proceedings.) The non-fainters bowed at me then went to the back of the queue. As queuing went, it was all rather efficient, but as they were all identical I had no idea whether I was meeting new hamsters or whether they were just going round in circles!

"Cookies!" Martha suddenly shouted from her room, no doubt dreaming about her favourite food.

The hamsters shot off. I tried to follow them into the hallway, but they moved too fast. I was just quick enough to see the last of the hamsters disappear down the stairs.

Where could they be coming from? Back in my room, the only sign of their visit was a smattering of poos on the floor, shelves, lampshade – well, you name it! I gathered up the poos and flushed them down the toilet. This, of course, disturbed Dad, who called out while I was thoroughly washing my hands.

"That you, Olly? Midnight wee?"

"Poo actually," I responded truthfully.

> Chatroom for Alien Contact

WeAreNotAlone65: PLEASE tell me someone else's scanners registered that? Not only am I getting a glitchy, unrecognized signal going from somewhere near MY house up into space, last night, possibly not for the first time, SOMETHING RESPONDED. I haven't quite managed to trace the source of the signal but, according to my devices, it was on the exact opposite route as the previously detected messages. This is a lot to take in. You read it here first, folks – I'm a whisker away from becoming the first human to prove the existence of aliens among us.

I'm so pleased Alien Con XXV is just around the corner. I need to be among true believers at this exciting time.

TangerineDream: My eyes are open.

PartKlingon99: I'm still banned for the next five Alien Cons. That's what happens when you learn the truth. You get SILENCED. Tread carefully, my friend. I wish someone had given me that advice after my

CHAPTER EIGHT

I went back to bed, but there was absolutely NO WAY I was going to be able to sleep. Somehow, I needed to encourage the hamsters back. As I waited for Dad to definitely be asleep again, a plan formed in my mind. As soon as I could hear him snoring, I tiptoed downstairs and looked for things I could give the hamsters as snacks – it seemed the least I could do when they had spent so much time, erm, *bowing* to me.

I found plenty of fruit and veg, as well as cheese, which I knew was a favourite snack for them. I filled a few bowls with tasty treats and was just in the process of chopping up a Granny Smith when I sensed I wasn't alone.

Slowly, I turned around. All over the kitchen, there were possibly EVEN more hamsters. Tibbles popped up on the worktop, paused to bow to me, and again started squeaking at the others. The hamsters started swaying and creating this weird noise all together, almost like they were chanting. This was even stranger than the bowing, so I encouraged them towards the bowls of food as a distraction, which I placed on the floor.

The food disappeared faster than I could replace it. I searched the cupboards for seeds, nuts and anything else I could remember from my "List of foods for Sharon". Even though they were small, there were lots of hamsters and they appeared to be VERY hungry. I couldn't believe how much they were eating. When there was no more food to give, I opened the back door and the hamsters streamed out into the garden. I was thankful that Dad's and Martha's bedrooms were both at the front of the house. I unlocked Martha's pink, plastic, shell-shaped sandpit and eased open the lid (yes, for safety reasons, my dad keeps the sandpit locked). The hamsters piled into it, squeaking in delight and, in the moonlight, I could see them swimming through the sand like it was water.

I found Tibbles and held out my hand for him to climb on to. I took him over to the part-demolished trampoline.

"Was this something to do with you, little guy?" I asked him, feeling rather foolish for accusing a tiny hamster of damaging my trampoline.

In response, Tibbles squeaked over and over again, his black box repeating "Tibbles". The hamster raised his paws as if pointing to the sky, then down to the trampoline and finally at the hedge. He was definitely trying to tell me something.

As he squeaked, seeds fell from his mouth on to my palm. No wonder the food had disappeared so quickly – the hamsters had all filled their cheek pouches!

But after a minute of watching Tibbles, I was no closer to working out what he was saying. I looked back into the house and saw what a mess we'd created – upturned bowls everywhere, empty packets strewn about, nut shells scattered over the sofa. With a sigh, I returned Tibbles to the sandpit and left the hamsters to play while I started the lonely job of clearing up.

Moments later, a hissing pierced the

air and I saw Tibbles, raised up on an upturned bucket, communicating with the other hamsters and gesticulating wildly. He seemed mightily displeased. And then, before my very eyes, the hamsters all filed back into the house and ... started clearing up!

Imagine the scene in *Cinderella* or *Snow White* (not that I've watched them recently, but Martha is a bit obsessed and when they are on, I can't help but glance at the screen sometimes) where cute, fluffy woodland creatures help the main fairy-tale characters with cleaning and tidying. That's basically what happened to me, but this was no fairy tale. After locking the back door, I just stood and gawped as Tibbles squeaked instructions from the breakfast bar and the hamsters worked in harmony to shift around bowls, sweep up crumbs, work the tap and use their fur to dry the dishes. Several were even on poo duty, carefully picking up all the little pellets and piling them on the coffee table. I was not a hundred per cent certain of their hygiene levels but, by the end, everything looked tidy enough. I'd just stood there in disbelief, not wanting to move and accidentally squish a hamster underfoot. I still had no idea what was happening or why, but these hamsters seemed to be quite keen on me and splatting a couple of them with a mistimed step would probably lessen their devotion.

Just as the final bowl was being lifted back into the cupboard by what can only be described as a hamster pyramid, a light flicked on upstairs, casting long shadows down the stairs. We all froze (well, I was frozen before, so I guess I continued to freeze).

"Hello?" Dad called quietly.

I could see the top hamster still holding the bowl in its front paws, struggling under its weight. The pyramid started to wobble. I tried to dive for the bowl but – too late – the pyramid collapsed, and the hamsters spilled off the worktop and over the floor. The bowl slipped to the floor and smashed.

"That's it. I know you're down there. You'd better start to run," warned Dad, although this threat was so unconvincing, if I had been a burglar, I might have laughed. As Dad's son, however, I *was* pretty scared. How was I supposed to explain all the hamsters? I wasn't even allowed to bring Sharon home for one weekend and here I was, about to be caught having the hamster party of the year! A slippered foot appeared on the top step and, with that, all the hamsters shot off.

"All OK, Olly?" asked Dad, clearly relieved but seeing me in a state of confusion, surrounded by broken pieces of bowl.

"Erm," I managed. "I was hungry so was making myself a snack, but the bowl slipped. I'm sorry."

"Are you still hungry?" asked Dad when he'd finished clearing up the broken pieces of bowl, while insisting I stay very still.

He opened the fridge and looked somewhat surprised at the lack of food, especially considering our groceries had been delivered the day before. Then he opened a cupboard to find it nearly empty.

"Olly, you seem to have already had

your snack." He gave me a concerned look. "Overeating is not a good thing, even if you are a growing lad. You see what happens when you miss breakfast!"

What was I supposed to say? I mumbled something about trying to have more control in future, which seemed to do the job. I was about to head upstairs when I spotted, tucked behind the breakfast bar and very much visible if Dad followed me, Tibbles and about thirty other hamsters. Tibbles seemed to be pointing to something on the coffee table. I looked more closely and realized it was the rather large collection of hamster poos.

I had several immediate problems:

- helping Tibbles and the trapped hamsters disappear to wherever the other hamsters had gone,

- trying to get Dad upstairs without noticing said hamsters,
- getting rid of the hamster poo pile.

I saw the open sandpit through the back door and inspiration struck.

"Did you know the sandpit is open, by the way, Dad?"

"What? That deathtrap?" Dad said, alarmed. "I'm sure I closed it earlier. Thanks for noticing, Olly." He unlocked the back door and ducked out.

This was the moment that Tibbles and crew could make their escape. I gestured at them to flee – which they did (after one or two bows). I quickly tried to snatch up the pile of poos, but without having time to form a better plan, I had to shove the handful in my dressing gown pocket just as Dad came back inside.

"Oh, is that one remaining crumb for me, Olly?" asked Dad, whose eagle eyes had spotted a single hamster poo.

He reached past me to pick it up.

"NO!" I shouted, and whacked it out of his hands. "I'd, err, I'd dropped that one on the floor."

Dad eyed me with suspicion.

"OK, thanks," he said. "Don't want to be eating floor crumbs, do we? Think of the germs!"

Ah, thank goodness for Dad's health and safety hang-ups!

Everything in order, Dad followed me back upstairs and, with each step, I could feel my pocket of hamster poo bang gently against my thigh.

From Tibbles, Mission Lead for the Faithful on Operation O

To Fluffy the 1000th, the Great and Most Fluffisome, Tender-Hearted Leader of Hamsters

Date HCT 172,471

Most Tender-Hearted Leader,

Tonight, we witnessed the kindness of the divine O. He is great indeed. As what I assume was a reward for our beliefs, we witnessed the miracle of the Most Delicious Food – or MDF, as it will be known, when I write the new chapters for The Stories on our return to the colony. Foods that no hamster from our colony has ever experienced. Do you know that food can actually *taste good*? That it can do more than fill our stomachs and provide much-needed energy? This nectar with which we were treated by Him was on a whole other level. I know you were happy to feel His presence by orbiting Earth in our Mothership, but what a shame you are not here to meet Him directly. You truly are a generous leader, allowing others to experience this in your stead. I shall make sure I bring you back the biggest orbs of blue juiciness (my favourite) when we return.

More proof of His goodness lies in the fact that He shares His home with the tyrant known as Martha. We must avoid her at all costs. She keeps the hideously wizened elder hostage with regular tantrums, eased only by the giving of round spotty food known as "cookies", which I imagine must contain a potion of some kind to soothe her. "Dad" is treated as a servant by Martha. Perhaps this is a test for him? Or a punishment? He does everything for her. The only respite he appears to get is when they take her to "nursery". He even has the undignified task of wiping Martha's bottom, as she poos straight into a parcel that she wears, which makes the process a lot more smeary. I do wonder why humans have such smeary poo – they should plop out neat little nuggets like we do. So much simpler. AND Martha's dad even has to congratulate and thank Martha for the poo. So sad to see.

You see, we are learning many things from our time on Earth. I hope to be reunited with you soon, to share both knowledge and MDF with your most tender-hearted self.

Your servant,

Tibbles

CHAPTER NINE

The next morning, Dad didn't mention my midnight feast or the broken bowl, but I could feel him watching me as I chomped down my Crunchy Golden Nobbles. Rather than the delicious crunchy nobbliness I usually enjoyed, my cereal suddenly seemed so very dry.

My brain fizzed with the excitement of the night before, but guilt pressed down on my chest. I wasn't sure how I was going to last the whole weekend this way. There was one person who could help me: Stan.

After breakfast, while Dad chased Martha around, trying to put a nappy on her as she refused to stay still, I used the distraction to ring Stan. I blurted out as much as I could about the night before, determined for Stan to take my hamster story seriously this time.

"... and then they tidied up, and then they broke a bowl and then Dad nearly ate a hamster poo, and I'm lying to Dad all the time now and I don't know what to do." I finished.

Silence on the other end.

"Stan?"

A long breath whistled down the phone.

"So, hamsters basically *tidied the house* for you?" he eventually said.

"*That's* your main takeaway from everything?" I was pleased that Stan definitely appeared to believe me about the hamsters this time, but he seemed to be focusing on the wrong thing.

"Of course. It's AWESOME. Do you know what this means?" asked Stan. Even though I couldn't see him, I could tell from his voice he had a cheeky glint in his eye. "You could probably get them to do ANYTHING you wanted. You have a willing army of hamster servants. Just think what you could do with that!"

"I don't want to think what I can do with an army of hamster servants," I said. Stan might have been impressed with this idea, but I couldn't for the life of me think what an army of hamsters could be used for. All I was thinking about was the stress of having to keep them secret. And all that hamster poo. And the lying. And especially the poo. What could be enjoyable about this weird development in my life? Why couldn't

I be more like Stan? "I need your help with this."

"OK. But it might involve some more … untruths to your dad. At least to start with," said Stan. "Get more hamster snacks in – I'm coming for a sleepover. But first you're going to meet me at Scarphall Pet Emporium this afternoon."

What? What on earth did we need with a pet shop? I needed *fewer* hamsters, not *more*!

After my hamster-filled night, I didn't have the energy to question Stan's plan – at least he had one – but his mum was far more easy-going than my dad and, as Stan said, if I was going to get his help, it involved yet more lying to Dad. Task one was to come up with a reason for Stan to come for a sleepover that evening. Even though Dad liked Stan, he was never keen on sleepovers as they "ruined the chance of an optimal night's sleep" so there always needed to be a good reason for one. I made up a maths test for the Monday morning, which seemed to do the job. Task two was to get more snacks. I knew Dad would never go for a midnight feast idea, but I seriously needed to replace all the fruit and veg the hamsters had devoured the night before, especially if they were going to appear again, so requested that we buy in lots of "brain food" to help me and Stan with our revision. Dad was delighted by my sudden interest in healthy eating.

Getting to a pet shop was the real problem. Dad was funny about all pets, not just hamsters. When I added a request to meet Stan at Scarphall Pet Emporium, Dad was on the brink of refusing when I blurted out:

"It's for a test on Monday morning."

Dad's eyebrows shot up.

"You have *two* tests on Monday morning?"

Ah, bum. I'd already used that lie. I was in deep now.

"Yes. On, err, pet care."

"Miss Harper seems to be working you very hard, considering you're nearly at the end of term. I should maybe have a word, don't you think?" Dad offered.

"I think that will be it for tests," was all I could think of saying in response. Hopefully no further hamster emergencies would require me to make up non-existent tests. The last thing I needed was Dad coming into school to have a go at Miss Harper.

Dad seemed to accept this and that afternoon, after a trip to the supermarket for healthy food (plus cookies for Martha, who sat in her car seat eyeing them greedily as they lay in the bag on my lap on top of the fart-smelling veg), we pulled up outside Scarphall Pet Emporium, where Stan was already waiting.

Dad was all ready to get out of the car with Martha to come into the pet shop with us, but I had a plan for this. As I jumped out of the car, I handed Martha her new box of cookies, to squeals of delight. Dad wasn't going anywhere! I dashed over to Stan, who was twirling around a lamp post. "Olly! Not so fast," Dad shouted out of his car window.

Oh no. So close.

He beckoned me back over. I had no idea what Stan wanted with the pet shop, but I was fairly sure that Dad's presence would not help the situation.

"How do you expect to learn anything without taking notes?"

Dad handed me a pencil and notebook from the glove box in his car – phew.

The pet shop smelled of a mixture of hay, rubber and, to be honest, my house. Or was my house starting to smell like a pet shop? As we entered, I tried to find out from Stan exactly why we were there.

"Don't you have questions?" he said. "Don't you want to know where the hamsters have come from and why they are at yours?"

"Yes."

We were approaching the pet shop owner. Oh no. Did Stan actually expect me to *talk* to this person?

"Go on then," said Stan. He shoved me forward encouragingly. "Ask your questions."

Ha! It was like he didn't know me at all. I stepped back and looked pleadingly at Stan, tilting my head in the woman's direction. Stan sighed but he did at least take pity on me.

The owner of the pet shop, who introduced herself as Ginny, looked quite alarmed when Stan asked if they'd lost any hamsters recently. She hurried over to the wall of glass cabinets and did a quick check.

"Nope. All present and correct – we generally stock up to ten at a time."

As directed by me (in a whisper), Stan asked Ginny about where she sourced her hamsters – but she was not willing to tell us. Adults are strange. I put my hand to Stan's ear and told him to say we were doing a school project on hamsters. At this point she opened up a bit – I think she had been worried we were going to open a hamster shop and put her out of business!

"Ask her about dwarf hamsters!" I tried to whisper into Stan's ear, but I overbalanced and ended up actually making contact – my lips on Stan's lobe. At this point, Stan walked off, wiping his wet ear with his shoulder, leaving Ginny, who had clearly heard my question, to explain that she didn't know anywhere locally that sold the smaller hamsters.

A fail, then.

And now there was no getting away from the fact that I was dangerously close to having a direct conversation with an adult. She was looking at me expectantly and I realized that she'd asked me a question – not that I'd heard it, thanks to the loud pounding in my ears. I broke eye contact and stared intently at a squeaky toy in the shape of a sprout like it was the most interesting item in the shop.

Ginny still stood there, expecting an answer. Thankfully Stan saved me.

"Oi, Olly, over here."

Stan was standing by the wall of hamster glass boxes. I joined him. He grabbed my shoulders and moved me directly in front of a hamster cage, then stepped back, watching.

"What are you doing?" I asked.

"Just seeing. I thought maybe these hamsters would start bowing. Or burst into song. Or do a little dance in your honour."

"Very funny." The hamsters had not batted an eyelid at my presence.

"What about other animals?" Stan was on a roll now.

He paraded me around the pet shop, stationing me in front of rabbits, gerbils, guinea pigs, a gecko, some stick insects and a whole spectrum of fish.

"Well, you don't seem to hold any special interest to them, either," Stan concluded, his eyes narrowing, as if he was starting to doubt my story again.

"You have to see *my* hamsters. Hundreds of hamsters all following me around and bow—"

Stan suddenly coughed and nodded his head at something behind me. I turned around and saw Ginny looking rather confused at what she had overheard.

"We're practising for the school play," Stan explained. I was impressed that Stan had come up with an excuse so easily and smoothly. By contrast, I was just holding my head in my hands. "Erm, it's a new version of Shakespeare's *Hamlet* – but we're doing, erm, *Hamster-let*. It's a hamster-based play."

OK, so maybe it wasn't particularly easy or smooth, but Ginny accepted it enough to go back to the counter.

Stan turned to me. "Well, I think we've

made some discoveries here. We know that none of the animals in here find you remotely interesting. So now it's time for stage two: show me the hamsters!"

NEWSFLASH

From Fluffy the 1000th, the Great and Most
Fluffisome Tender-Hearted Leader of Hamsters

As I sit, bravely orbiting the planet known as Earth, the
supposed place of origin of our colony's founders, I worry
for our band of hamsters down there. The landing party has
met with difficulty, and it is my duty to prepare you to expect
the worst. We knew this would be a dangerous mission and,
instead of triumphantly returning with concrete evidence of
O's existence, I fear that Tibbles and the other faithful may be
lost to us for ever on a barren, unforgiving planet. If so, we will
have to face a lot of uncomfortable questions about our history,
and what we've come to believe for so many years about O.

I will continue my vigil and report further developments. And
know that I, Fluffy the 1000th, the Great and Most Fluffisome,
your one true master, will be doing everything I can to
bring our fellow hamsters home.

CHAPTER TEN

Stan was not best pleased to have to practise maths for a made-up test as part of our sleepover.

"You could have said we were working on our science fair project," he complained. "At least that's something we actually need to do. It's coming up *this week*."

Ooops! Stan might have been right, but my lies had led to an evening of maths revision and that was that. And anyway, I was refusing to even think about the science fair. Some pupils in our class had been working away on their projects for the whole term, while many, including Stan and me, hadn't even started. I had been avoiding the idea of the science fair because how was I supposed to compete with Dad's school legacy? I knew the teachers were hoping that I would suddenly be like Dad, the legendary best-ever pupil. As if! To have that expectation hanging over my head was intimidating, as was having Dad's old science project ACTUALLY hanging over our heads in the school hall. His Space Capsule 2 was the benchmark all science projects had been judged against ever since. What was the point in even trying? Besides, we had a fake maths test to pretend to revise for.

So, that evening after tea, while Dad took Martha up to bed, me and Stan settled down to some revision. I had hoped that this would make us look like well-behaved boys with no intention of entertaining hundreds of hamsters that very evening. Unfortunately, I hadn't considered Dad's reaction to this – when he came back down, he was overjoyed to see me attempting some maths. He hovered in the background distractingly while we went over the same calculation again and again. I was *just* starting to get it when Dad offered his assistance (or should I say *expertise*). Dad might be a science genius but by the time he'd finished his explanation, he was talking about quantum physics and quarks and I was left questioning whether the number one actually meant one any more. It was hopeless. If anything, Stan looked even more confused than I was feeling – he certainly wasn't looking like his usual confident self.

At nine p.m., Dad sent us upstairs to

bed, so all we had to do was wait for him to go to sleep. It took AGES but, eventually, silence fell over the house. Stan and I grabbed our healthy snacks and tiptoed down to the main room, leaving the stair gates open for a hasty retreat if needed. As we reached the bottom step, I could see all the hamsters dotted around the room and Tibbles chattering to them from the kitchen counter. When they saw me, they began their bowing, swaying and weird chanting. Then they froze when they saw Stan with me.

"That's amazing," whispered Stan, his eyes as wide as flying saucers. "I'm trying not to be freaked out by this."

We carefully moved forward. With each step, hamsters moved out of our way.

By the time we'd put the snacks out, the hamsters had got used to Stan, and they flooded towards the food. We stepped gingerly over to the sofa and, when it looked safe to do so, flopped down on it.

Stan started stroking his chin, deep in thought. "Do you think I can have a go? Commanding them, I mean?"

"I don't really command them. I still have no idea how much they understand. Mainly they just copy me or do what Tibbles tells them – but fill your boots."

"OK, here goes." Stan stood up confidently. "Hamsters, erm, copy me."

Stan proceeded to make various movements, including what appeared to be a version of "Heads, shoulders, knees and toes". He really threw himself into it. And not one hamster paid any attention. They were just filling their cheek pouches and watching me as usual.

"Bad luck, Stan. Apparently, you just don't have my level of charm!" I grinned.

"We know *that* isn't true. There HAS to be a reasonable explanation," said Stan.

I got up from the sofa and started refilling the already-empty bowls. The sea of hamsters followed behind me, ready.

"All I keep thinking, and I know this sounds completely bonkers." I paused, knowing what I was about to say *really was* bonkers. But if I couldn't tell my best friend, who could I tell? "I have been a *really good* hamster classroom monitor this year. I just wonder if somehow, somewhere, someone knows that, and this is my reward. Does that sound ridiculous?"

"Karma! That's not ridiculous. Loads of people believe that if you do good things, good things happen."

I breathed more easily and felt my body relax.

Stan continued, "You're right. The way

these hamsters act around you, it's like they think you're their god."

OK, Stan had taken my bonkers theory and topped it with an even more ludicrous one.

"Think about it. They follow you around. They do what you say. You have provided food and water, which they probably think are, like, miracles or something. You've got your own little hamster cult! Amazing! Olly Brown, god of hamsters! Lord of hamsters. Hamster Man! That's hilarious!"

Stan doubled over laughing at the idea.

"Hey, cut it out," I said. "I get the picture."

"Aww, spoilsport! That's no way for the legendary leader of hamsters to talk, is it? Oo, oo, oo – I know – you are the Master of the Hamsterverse!"

"Yeah, OK. Very funny."

I flopped back down on the sofa and sighed.

"But what if you're right?" I asked. "What on earth do they want from ME? And why me?" I watched some of the hamsters work together to place one of Martha's empty plastic bowls back in the cupboard and made a mental note to try to remember to clean it properly before her breakfast. "Looking after a whole bunch of hamsters is stressful, you know. Imagine what Dad would do if he found them. And what if they all start following me around all the time, at school and stuff? Tibbles has already been to school twice. And then there's Meddling Martha, who's already eaten at least four hamster poos."

"How did—" started Stan.

"That's not important right now," I

interrupted. "I'd just rather not be leader of hamsters or whatever you want to call it. All I wanted was to be allowed to take Sharon home for a weekend, possibly with a view to being allowed my very own hamster at some point. Not dozens of hamster disciples!"

Stan shook his head. "Oh, Olly, Olly, Olly. Typical Olly. You're looking at this all wrong. This shouldn't be *stressful*. It should be AWESOME. You have a devoted group of hamsters who will do whatever you want. So..."

He looked at me expectantly.

"What?"

"So, what do you want? If you could wish for something to be done for you? To be better at something? Think of it. Name it. Nothing could be too outlandish."

I had no idea if he was right, but Stan

did have a point. Maybe I *had* been looking at the situation wrong.

"I have no idea."

We watched as the hamsters finished munching away and then, it must be said, very responsibly cleared up after themselves and scampered out into the garden. I'd unlocked Martha's sandpit earlier, and they dove in, chattering with glee.

I turned to Stan. "So, if you were in my position, what would you do?"

"Parp," buzzed in Stan, like I'd got an answer wrong on a TV game show. "Nope. *Your* hamster cult. *Your* ideas. What do YOU want?"

He wasn't making this easy for me. He picked up his maths book and pencil, flicked to the back and looked at me expectantly.

"Well." My eyes rested on Martha's safety gate on the stairs, and something occurred to me. "Ever since Martha came along, Dad has been more over the top than ever about safety. I mean, I love Martha and everything, but she's also a real pain and life was definitely simpler before. I can't exactly say 'Please get rid of Martha', can I?"

"Hmmm," mused Stan, as if it wasn't the worst idea. "It's a start. I'm writing it down."

I watched as he wrote down GET RID OF MARTHA, tongue sticking out of his mouth as he scribbled. Tibbles appeared next to us on the top of the sofa and started squeaking, but I was focused on Stan.

"Come on, though. What else?"

I racked my brains. Minutes ticked by.

"This is daft," I said. "What can tiny little hamsters actually do?"

"You don't know because you haven't

tried," said Stan. "You *always* limit yourself that way too. Just think – maybe these hamsters can handle weapons. Maybe we can work out how to communicate with them. *Maybe* they can even rise up to form one massive uber hamster."

"In what situation would I need weapon-toting hamsters? Can you give me an example?"

"Erm…"

"Exactly."

"*Olly?*"

"What are they going to do? Be my bodyguards? Suddenly give me confidence to talk in class? Make me popular? Get rid of Hugh? All these thi—"

"Olly! Look!" Stan pointed to the stairs.

I spun round and gasped.

There, floating down the stairs, was

Martha, fast asleep! Underneath her, hundreds of hamsters were working together like a furry conveyor belt. Incredible! I stood up and gawped. Then I realized what I'd said and what the hamsters were intending to do.

"No! No! Stop! I don't *actually* want to get rid of Martha. Stop this! Take her back upstairs before she wakes up."

The hamsters paused, looking to Tibbles for instructions. Tibbles looked at me. The hamsters looked at Tibbles.

"Take her back upstairs," I repeated.

Nothing.

"I think these little chaps can do more than you give them credit for," said Stan, tapping his maths book.

"You wrote it down! I'm not sure Tibbles understands when

I speak, but you wrote that down! Tibbles can read!"

I grabbed the book from Stan and wrote: TAKE MARTHA BACK TO BED.

I showed the message to Tibbles, who squeaked and gesticulated. Seconds later the conveyor belt reversed, carrying the still-sleeping Martha back up the stairs.

What a breakthrough! Tibbles could read!

I wrote down WHAT DO YOU WANT? Tibbles chattered away but all I could hear still was "Tibbles, Tibbles, Tibbles" coming out of his black box. I had no idea how to stop this from being a one-way conversation. At least I knew to be careful about what was written down – I couldn't risk accidentally throwing away my little sister again!

"So, thanks to me," said Stan, eyes shining, "we've found a way for them to understand you. So now you can ask them to do stuff for you. This is amazing!"

"Maybe so," I said.

Perhaps there was more that these hamsters could do for me. I just needed to find out what!

From Tibbles, Mission Lead for the Faithful on Operation O

To Fluffy the 1000th, the Great and Most Fluffisome, Tender-Hearted Leader of Hamsters

Date HCT 172,472

Most Tender-Hearted Leader,

A breakthrough! I am able to read O's writings, so I am now able to receive His instructions. I have not yet worked out a way to ask Him the favour we need of Him, but our belief in Him will surely lead to a miracle: the miracle of retrieving our spaceship.

At least this gives me more opportunity to observe O and the humans. The front paws of the humans are engaged in a wide variety of ways. Like us, they use their front paws for eating - but the humans do not have the ability to store food in cheek pouches, so they waste a lot of time putting food into their mouths. They also use their front paws to hold up their communication devices, which seems like a bad design. Even in the short time I have been observing them, I see them walk into each other with remarkable regularity. This appears to be a new development since the time of the Ancient Ones, as nothing of this kind is reported in the Scriptures. I worry that humans no longer have time for looking after animals and gazing into the cosmos, as O had done long ago.

I hope you are continuing to receive my messages, despite my faulty communications device. I am certain we will soon retrieve the spaceship and be able to complete the mission - have faith.

Your servant,

Tibbles

CHAPTER ELEVEN

Stan left on Sunday morning, glad to escape
before Dad started us off with yet more
maths revision, but I had promised to think
hard about what I could get the hamsters to
do for me. Perhaps Stan was right and this
was a fantastic opportunity. Knowing that
Tibbles could read made my life so much
easier, although I could still only guess what
he was trying to tell *me*. During Sunday,
secretly shut in my bedroom, I tried to see
if he could write, but giving him a pencil
led to him over-balancing and flipping on

to his back like the world's most rubbish pole-vaulter. Still unable to find my pencil sharpener, I broke off the pencil's lead, but even though Tibbles's adorable claws seemed perfectly developed for holding a tiny pencil, all he drew were circles. Endless circles.

I also tried to get Tibbles to type, but that was even less successful, unless you understand what the message asdkchgbwwwwwshipFEBLWIHYCOEDv means? We went back to the broken lead, because at least Tibbles was trying to communicate *something* with the circles – but what?

Ultimately, with my promise to Stan ringing in my ears, I didn't want to waste time deciphering the circular scribblings – it was time to enjoy myself! Sadly, this turned out to be easier said than done. After three nights of hamster entertaining, I was starting to feel exhausted. I jumped at any strange noise and my nostrils permanently sensed a hamstery whiff, like I'd just wiped my nose with one. Other than Tibbles, the hamsters had only appeared at night, but that didn't reassure me. It would have helped to know where they disappeared off to – where they were actually living. I found myself patrolling all corners of my home, looking out for evidence of hamster activity. What if they started chewing wires?

Sunday night zapped any remaining energy I had. Even though the nightly hamster entertaining had eased into a routine of bowing, snacks, bowing, sandpit, bowing, tidying and, for good measure, lots more bowing, I was too tired to enjoy any of it. If anything, there seemed to be EVEN MORE hamsters. I sat motionless on the sofa, staring into space with Tibbles next to me, while the others played around us. I was holding a notepad and pencil but did not have the brain power to think of any useful questions. In the end, I wrote:

Make sure you tidy up. I'm going to bed.

***

It was almost a relief to return to school on Monday, although Dad wished me luck for my maths and pet care tests as he kissed me goodbye, which reminded me of what a rubbish son I was being. It didn't help that, stashed in my bag, was Tibbles, who had appeared and climbed into my school bag before I could stop him. At least it was just the one hamster!

I spotted Stan and dragged him to a corner of the playground in order to show him Tibbles in my rucksack. As I described

Sunday night, Stan was looking across the playground. I *thought* he was looking out to make sure we weren't being overheard.

"I'm sure there were even more of them, Stan. They were on every surface," I said.

"Every *her face*," Stan echoed moonily.

Wait, what?

I glanced up. Stan wasn't listening to me at all! He was actually gazing, as if in a trance, at … Amelia Fletcher. Urgh! Horrendous Hugh's number one fan? What was going on?

But then the bell went for the day to start. I'd have to try and get Stan's attention properly at break time. My hamster issues were far more important than *Amelia Fletcher*.

At least hamsters can climb ropes.

***

I was so determined to talk to Stan at break time – AKA Sharon care time – that I passed him a note during our first lesson.

Secrets? Lies? *Note passing?* I was on a slippery slope.

Stan, knowing how out of character this was, took my note seriously, and by break time had somehow gained permission from Miss Harper, who that day was looking like a walking cactus in a floor-length ribbed green cardigan smattered with pink flowers, to stay in with me.

As soon as we were alone, I went to get Tibbles from my drawer – but there was no sign of him. Thankfully, I didn't have to search too hard. We found him next to Sharon's cage.

"Does he always have that dreamy look on his face?"

Stan was right. I'd not really noticed

Tibbles looking like that before – all dewy-eyed and full of wonder – except for the first time I had seen him, in that exact same spot. In fact, the look in Tibbles's eyes reminded me of the look on Stan's face in the playground that morning...

As we watched, Tibbles reached into his mouth and pulled out a chunk of apple, a chunk of cheese, and a pawful of seeds. He placed each item of food in the sleeping Sharon's cage.

"Oooh! I think *someone's* got the hots for Sharon!" Stan said.

Yes. Poor Tibbles was smitten. And Sharon, who was about four times his size and could probably swallow him whole, didn't even acknowledge the gifts of food. Poor little guy.

But, if Tibbles was in love with Sharon, did that mean that *Stan* fancied *Amelia*?

I shook that thought right out of my head.

"It's not his love life I'm worried about," I said. "I'm really struggling with all the hamsters. I know you want me to enjoy having them around but I'm just tired and stressed."

"These hamsters are wasted on you. Thankfully, you have me to show you the way," said Stan. "I'd have at least seen if they could carry me, like they carried Martha down the stairs. Or got them to clean my room, or something."

Together, we tried to think of any ways the hamsters could be of use. We thought about the different events coming up at school.

"How about Sports Day?" asked Stan. "Couldn't you do something for that?"

"Like what, exactly? We can't have all the pupils, parents and teachers watching me be carried along the track on a sea of hamsters. They'd all see – you know – the hamsters. And me not actually running."

Sports Day was out. We looked further down our timetable.

"What about our trip to the seaside on Friday? I could maybe take them along. They'd love the sandy beach."

Stan thought about this for a second. "But what would *you* get out of that? Giving them a nice day out is fine, but where's the benefit for you?"

It was hopeless. The way I saw it, the hamsters, however cute and fluffy they were, were causing me nothing but hassle.

"I just want to get through this week," I found myself saying. "Maybe the hamsters will leave and things can just go back to normal."

"Can't we at least do something for the science fair?" asked Stan. "Come on. You're the hamster expert slash god. Can't we use that somehow? You could claim to have trained a group of hamsters and demonstrate the hamsters following you around and copying you. That'd look so amazing."

It was easy to see where Stan was coming from, but showing the world (or, to start with, my school) my hamster powers was not something I wanted. Not only would this have meant me answering LOTS of questions, most of which I didn't know the answers to, it would also mean me being very close to the centre of attention. And how would my dad take the news that I was now Lord of Hamsters, or whatever Stan wanted me to call myself? No. The hamsters had to remain secret.

From Tibbles, Mission Lead for the Faithful on Operation O

To Fluffy the 1000th, the Great and Most Fluffisome, Tender-Hearted Leader of Hamsters

Date HCT 172,474

Most Tender-Hearted Leader,

The devine O does seem keen to understand me, but all attempts so far are proving fruitless. He did provide me with something I could use to draw – but sadly He did not appear to comprehend my pictures of our planet, the black hole, the bouncy object at our landing site or the large round pond where our spaceship currently resides. Perhaps I need more practice drawing them.

O shows great kindness to the special hamster he visits daily – the vision of loveliness I mentioned in a previous communication of mine. She is unlike any hamster I have ever seen. So big and so fluffy (though not the Most Fluffisome, as no hamster can claim that title save you, most glorious leader). I am glad to accompany O on his daily routines, though the rest of the faithful are also keen to start following O around more. I fear I can only prevent them for so long.

A thought has struck me. The humans have lots of different kinds of vehicles. I know, unlike their food, their technology is not as advanced as ours, but perhaps there is a spaceship here we could use to return to our colony? We only need a little rocket to get back to you on the Mothership. Maybe we don't need the submerged ship after all – I will report back.

Your servant,

Tibbles

From Fluffy the 1000th, the Great and Most Fluffisome,
Tender-Hearted Leader of Hamsters

To Tibbles, Servant

Date HCT 172,474

Oh, for the sake of all that is fluffy, you MUST get the spaceship. Do what you must to retrieve it. I need that spaceship. No other ship or vehicle will do. The spaceship is central to my plan.

The success of the mission depends on this.

Only contact me again when the spaceship is operational.

F

CHAPTER TWELVE

The rest of the week should have been busy and exciting but, in my exhausted state, with the nightly hamster entertaining still going on, I struggled to enjoy it. Tibbles continued to accompany me to school. He'd made himself a hidden area beside Sharon's cage, so he could be as close to her as possible. Each break, he retrieved love tokens from his cheek pouches for Sharon, who continued to ignore him, generally sleeping through his attempted courtship. Watching Tibbles change so much around Sharon, I started to closely watch Stan's reactions to Amelia. Sure enough, whenever she was about, Stan became less confident – less like himself. I was also becoming certain that the weird red thing he was crocheting was meant for Amelia.

Tuesday was Sports Day, where I sleepily stumbled through the 400-metre race (coming last) and then nearly got hit by a shot-put as *something* had distracted me in the long-jump sandpit. I could swear I'd seen a flash of gold. It was a sensation I was experiencing more and more – that flicker of movement out the corner of my eye. I knew exactly where Tibbles was, so what exactly was I seeing? Or maybe I was just so tired that my mind was playing tricks on me.

On Wednesday, Miss Harper gave me and Hugh the shocking (though nothing could be more shocking than the satsuma-orange cardigan with letterbox-red spots she was wearing – basically a headache in cardigan form) news that the Leavers' Party needed to be a bit less Hugh-focused and a bit more like a proper party – with games. I sat there uselessly as Hugh jabbered on about party games he could remember from all the parties he'd attended. I was rather at a disadvantage, having not been invited to any over my time at Burton Upper Primary School thanks to, well, him. My lack of knowledge, added to my dizzying tiredness, meant I struggled to concentrate and all I could think about was hamsters. Even any vague party games that swam into my mind were hamster-themed: pin the tail on the hamster; guess the number of hamster poos in a jar. Clearly, I had hamsters on the brain and I wasn't about to share these ridiculous party ideas with Hugh. I didn't need him to think I was bonkers. By the end of the afternoon, Hugh had made it quite clear he didn't want my help at all with the Leavers' Party, which I didn't really mind. However, that meant I definitely wouldn't be fulfilling my third target of speaking up and "making an impact" before the end of school.

It was on Wednesday too that Stan finally insisted we plan something for the science fair. This was only reasonable, I suppose, as it was taking place the next day. In the end, we agreed upon showing an experiment that Stan had seen online, where Skittles were placed on a plate with some water and the colours all run out, creating a beautiful rainbow effect. It was certainly no Space Capsule 2 – and I was fine with that. All I had to do was bring some Skittles to school the next day.

The science fair, to begin with at least,

turned out to be quite a lot of fun, especially if you like to see exploding volcanoes, which I do. Miss Harper, in a checked brown-and-lime-green cardigan, led some very lacklustre applause for the tenth volcano demonstration of the morning and announced, "*Finally*, we have something a bit different. Olly and Stan – over to you."

Stan got out the white plate he'd brought from home and readied a cup of water, while I went to get the Skittles from my bag. There was no sign of them. I searched and searched but found nothing.

Miss Harper was "very disappointed" in us, especially me. I had "let down the legacy" of my dad, apparently. Ugh. I was more bothered about having let Stan down. He had wanted to do *something* for the science fair – he really hadn't asked for much – but I'd even failed with that. I seemed to be failing a lot lately. The rest of the science fair continued, with Seren Simons showing part of a frog that she'd actually dissected. It was gross and Theo Redfern vomited over the floor. I was also feeling sick, but I think it was less to do with the frog guts and more to do with letting down my friend. I knew I'd *had* the Skittles in my bag – what had happened to them?

I didn't have to wait long to find out. At break, I saw Tibbles hiding as usual behind Sharon's cage. His face looked very puffed up and misshapen and, as I watched, he pushed some alarmingly bright coloured gifts into Sharon's cage. I snatched a piece of paper and scribbled:

Those were mine. They were for the science fair!

Tibbles looked up at me with dark, sorry eyes. I stormed away.

***

At the end of the day, I didn't even bother collecting Tibbles from school. I was sick of all hamsters. I even decided that, that night, I would focus on getting a good night's sleep, ready for the trip to the seaside the next day. I wasn't going to be doing any hamster entertaining – at all.

With my mind made up, I actually had a nice evening with Dad and Martha. I'd completely forgotten that every child in Hamster Class was supposed to take something along for the shared picnic the next day, but thankfully Dad had remembered and had bought all the ingredients for vegetarian sausage rolls. Dad chopped vegetables into tiny pieces and Martha stirred all the ingredients together. I was on pastry duty. It was lovely working together as a little team. Soon, the smell of buttery pastry filled the house.

I went to bed early, looking forward to the next day. After a while, a very sorry-looking Tibbles appeared.

IT'S OK, I wrote on the notepad I now kept ready by my bed. I was still annoyed at him, but there wasn't much I could do about the Skittles now. I sighed, looking at Tibbles's big, tear-filled eyes. Nothing was going as planned. I needed to give up this idea of being god of hamsters. I was so tired. In fact, I needed a break from hamsters, full-stop.

I wrote: *PLEASE STAY HERE TOMORROW*. I couldn't face having to secretly wrangle hamsters at the seaside, not even one. Tibbles squeaked sadly in response and scurried away.

> Chatroom for Alien Contact

WeAreNotAlone65: It's been three days now since I last picked up any signals. This is a tragedy – I truly believed this was it this time. I was finally on track to prove the existence of aliens among us and now – nothing. I'm not allowing myself to lose hope entirely as there is one possible explanation. There appears to be a strange reddish tint to my beloved pond. As we all know, ponds are key to encouraging alien engagement, so perhaps the discolouration is what is preventing me from picking up further signals. To fix the problem, I've booked someone to drain the pond. By the time I'm back from Alien Con XXV, all should be back to normal and I should be back to picking up extra-terrestrial communications.

DukeSkyHawker: Definitely the only logical explanation. Keep us posted.

PartKlingon99: Wish I could be there at Alien Con XXV but you know my feelings about it anyway. No one really wants to know the truth. Any notion that you really do have evidence and you will be silenced

CHAPTER THIRTEEN

I felt much better in the morning, but overslept, which meant I didn't have time for my Crunchy Golden Nobbles. I was actually looking forward to the class trip. A hamster-free day at the seaside was just what I needed, I thought, picking up the silver cool bag containing the vegetarian sausage rolls. Miss Harper had already told us the plan for the day – games on the beach, a ride on the big wheel and then lunch. On the coach, Stan tried to persuade her to let us spend some time in the amusements, but even his cheeky charm wasn't enough to get her to say yes.

"I was sure I'd win big on the slotties," he complained.

When we arrived at Crimplington, we piled out of the coach and everyone dumped their picnic dishes on a blanket laid out on the sand, while Miss Harper, in a turquoise-and-shocking-pink vertically-striped cardigan (possibly her most tasteful) set up the beach for cricket. While everyone was picking teams, I hung back, knowing I would be the last one chosen. My tummy gurgled from its lack of breakfast, so I decided to have a sausage roll early. I unzipped the cool bag and there, instead of thirty sausage rolls, were fifteen very full-looking hamsters, their cheeks bulging and golden pastry flakes sticking to their fur.

"What have you done?" I hissed at them. "Where's Tibbles?"

They all looked at me blankly with their beady black eyes. Of course they couldn't answer. They had no idea what I was saying. I poked around in the bag but couldn't see Tibbles anywhere.

"I guess we *have* to have Olly," I heard Hugh say. Great, now I was stuck in Horrendous Hugh's team too.

I continued to fume while the cricket game took place. Hugh stuck me way out at the boundary so I was not expected to *actually* take part in the game. I could see Stan on the other team standing awkwardly beside Amelia. Was he looking ... shy? That was my style, not his! I didn't understand what had got into Stan or how he could suddenly act so differently around someone – especially not Amelia. I eased my frustration by kicking around in the sand. I looked over at the picnic and realized that my silver cool bag, glinting in the sunshine, was still unzipped. I considered going over to zip it back up, but I didn't have time to act on that thought, because I heard …

"OLLLLLYYYYYYYY!"

… and looked up to find the cricket ball whizzing straight for me. By some miracle, I managed to catch it and was, for once, cheered by Hugh and half of the class. Hugh even smiled at me. Properly smiled! I'd caught out the other side's best batter and now it was our turn to bat.

The cricket game turned out to be quite a lot of fun and, thanks to my miracle catch, I was actually on the winning side for once. It was only after the game, as the class paired up to head over to the big wheel, that I was able to tell Stan about my hamster/sausage-roll disaster. I grabbed the cool bag and opened it to show him the guilty hamsters.

"Did you say fifteen hamsters? I can only count thirteen," said Stan, peering into the bag.

"There were *definitely* fifteen before," I said, snatching the cool bag away from Stan and investigating for myself. "Eleven, twelve, thirteen." My heart sank.

I zipped up the bag and carried it with me, determined that no other hamsters would escape. I hoped the missing two hamsters were somewhere close by, perhaps playing in the sand.

I could hear many of my classmates complaining as we rode on the Ferris wheel, especially as it gave us an excellent view of the Vomitator roller coaster and the Certain Death gravity ride, which they would rather have been on. I liked the calm movement of the big wheel. It felt safe and soothing and the view across the sea helped me forget my annoyance at the missing hamsters and my missing sausage rolls.

As we stepped off the big wheel, I suddenly noticed, on the metal tubing that formed the main circle of the wheel, two little golden shapes, running as if their lives depended on it.

"I think they've found the world's largest hamster wheel," I said to Stan, nodding my head in the direction of the hamsters. "You *have* to help me get to them."

I looked up and saw Miss Harper watching us suspiciously. There was absolutely no way I could get the hamsters back without her noticing. This was just so unfair. Finally, I was having a nice time with my class and the hamsters were *ruining* it, first by eating my lunch offering and now by being so ... irresponsible. I hadn't asked for this. In fact, I had expressly told Tibbles I didn't want any hamsters to come. I clenched my fists. They didn't deserve my help, but I couldn't just leave them on the big wheel. Miss Harper turned and started walking away, with the class following in pairs.

"Stan," I whispered as we joined the back of the crocodile, "please distract Miss Harper for me."

Stan looked very serious and gave a quick salute. Then he yelled "SLOTTIES" and ran into the closest amusement arcade. Miss Harper was definitely not amused and made chase, with the class following behind. I didn't have time to watch what happened next – I had hamsters to save.

I ducked behind the barrier, unnoticed by the bored, spotty student responsible for this massive, creaking bit of machinery. I climbed up a ladder and found myself at eye level to the curved, moving metal tube

where the hamsters were scurrying away, grins of pure glee on their faces. They were having the time of their lives, which made me *even more* annoyed. With one hand holding the ladder *and* my cool bag, I unzipped the bag with the other, feeling rather wobbly. Now, all I had to do was grab the hamsters and get them into the bag – without falling off the ladder!

Just then, I heard an ominous cawing sound and three massive seagulls swooped down. These brutes had spotted the hamsters and clearly decided this was their lunch. Still with one hand on the ladder, I waved around my other arm, trying to shoo the gulls away. I managed to grab one hamster, then the other. I shoved them into the cool bag but, just as I was starting down the ladder to safety, one of the gulls dived at me. I grabbed frantically at the ladder, but the cool bag fell to the ground below.

Quick as I could, I climbed down, but the gulls were quicker, and they sensed a tasty vegetarian sausage-roll-flavoured hamster snack was theirs for the taking. They took it in turns to peck at the still-open bag. I ran at them, screaming and jumping, arms open as wide as possible, punching in all directions. I was a teenager at a rock concert (or Martha having one of her meltdowns). This gave me enough time to grab the cool bag and zip it up. The gulls had missed their chance and flew off to snatch some chips from a gormless passer-by. Job done. I breathed a sigh of relief and looked around.

There, staring at me open-mouthed, was my entire class. Miss Harper, seething with anger, was gripping Stan's hand so tightly, I could see her knuckles turning white. I had no idea how long they'd been watching or how much they'd seen. I knew I needed to explain, which – nightmarishly – meant saying something to the entire class. I held up my silver cool bag.

"Vegetarian sausage roll?" I said.

***

Stan was in lots of trouble for his "disappearing" act, but I could tell Miss Harper knew Stan and I had been in cahoots. She just couldn't quite work out why. The rumour went around the class that I had been trying to save my sausage rolls from some vicious seagulls, which was almost true, so I was regarded by my classmates as some kind of hero, even though none of them wanted to eat a seagull-pecked sausage roll (thankfully). Things worked out better than they could have, but I was still livid with the hamsters. Enough was enough.

Back home, when everyone was in bed and the hamsters appeared downstairs, ready for snacks and playtime, I wrote a sign for Tibbles that read:

I WANT YOU ALL TO LEAVE

From Tibbles, Mission Lead for the Faithful on Operation O
To Fluffy the 1000th, the Great and Most Fluffisome, Tender-Hearted Leader of Hamsters
Date HCT 172,478

WE ARE BANISHED!

We have been sent away from the Divine O in disgrace. All we have done is try to praise Him and demonstrate our devotion. But we have displeased Him. We must now find our own solution to the spaceship problem. I am heartbroken.

I know you only wished to hear from me again when I had good news about the spaceship – but I felt it was important you knew about this development. I will try not to bother you again and humbly apologize if this contact bothers you further. It appears I have been doing lots of things wrong of late.

Never have I felt this low. Not even my faith is bringing me comfort.

My only solace at this time is being able to spend more time next to the hamster that I love.

Your servant,

Tibbles

CHAPTER FOURTEEN

The next morning, I could already tell that the hamsters were gone. The strange smell in my nostrils had faded and I could feel myself relax as I breathed in the fresher air. Even Martha's meltdown about a lack of cookies in the house didn't ruin my new calm. Dad and her dashed out on an emergency shopping trip, leaving me home alone.

It was very rare to be allowed to stay in the house by myself, so I enjoyed my time by lying on my bed, listening to the pure silence. No pittering. No pattering. Bliss!

Slowly, however, I became aware of noises outside my window. Not hamster noises, but something unusual. Odd enough for me to have a look.

There were strange goings-on in Mr Potter's garden. I don't mean the sign, angled up to the sky, that read "UFOs welcome here", or the plastic garden statues of aliens dotted around the shrubs, or the large string of fairy lights in the shape of flying saucers. I was used to seeing those things. No, I mean the man wearing what looked like over-sized plastic dungarees and a jacket that had "Pond-U-Like" scrawled across its back. He was wading in and out of Mr Potter's oddly red pond, looking very confused and exclaiming loudly. A bright yellow pipe was leading from the pond along the side passage, making gentle gurgling noises. There was no sign of Mr Potter.

As I watched, I could see that the water was going down and something was starting to emerge. The lower the water sank, the stranger the object in the centre of the pond appeared to be. It was an object unlike anything I'd ever seen. It was large – almost taking up the whole pond. From my bedroom window, I couldn't even tell what it was made of. It was cylindrical. Like a very wide, flat toilet roll. To be quite honest, it looked like a flying saucer. But that wasn't what I saw. No, what I saw, part-submerged in Mr Potter's pond, was a *giant hamster wheel*.

Could it possibly be hamster related? I thought back to the many times that Tibbles had pointed at the sky, then at the trampoline and then at Mr Potter's garden. Was I actually, genuinely considering the possibility that whatever was stuck in Mr Potter's pond had something to do with hamsters? Had Tibbles been trying to tell me they were – FROM SPACE?! Did hamsters from space make any less sense than me being worshipped by a colony of hamsters from Earth?

Before I could think properly, I was racing downstairs, out of the house and along the side passage into Mr Potter's garden, skipping carefully past the yellow pipe and ducking around a "I heart extra-terrestrials" sign. It was only when I reached the pond that I realized I was facing a difficult situation. I had to talk to an adult.

Yuck.

I had to think quickly.

"Hey!" I said, trying to sound casual and believable, but instead sounding like my voice had raised an octave. "That's where it went to! I can't believe *my school project* ended up in Mr Potter's pond. No wonder I couldn't find it!"

"You mean *you* made this?"

"Yes," I said. I pictured Stan's confidence with adults and tried my hardest to channel that by attempting a cheeky grin, but I fear I looked more like I was suppressing a fart.

"And it ended up here?"

"Well, clearly. I live next door." I pointed up to my bedroom. "I'm Olly."

"Hmmm. I'm Rich," said the man, looking from me to the two-metre-high hedge in disbelief. "You're telling me your school project somehow made it into the pond from your garden?"

"Erm, yes, that hedge actually provides no barrier at all and things go through it all the time. Erm. Footballs. This. My sister." I couldn't believe I was lying so easily – talking so easily, even. I think he was starting to buy it. "This is brilliant news. If you can help me get it out, maybe I can clean it up and still take it into school and Miss can change my fail mark into a pass."

"Well, son, you did lots of work on this … whatever it is. You surely deserve a pass. Come on then."

Rich strode back into the half-empty pond and started to push the object up. Standing in the water vertically, it looked even more like a hamster wheel. In that position, Rich was able to push it out of the pond and, between us, we rolled it along the side alley between the houses and up the passage to my garden. I couldn't think where else to put such a large object – for days I'd been hiding hundreds of hamsters in my house, but that was child's play compared to hiding a massive … well, whatever this was!

Short of options and time – I was sure Dad and Martha would be back soon – I decided to wheel it into Dad's shed. I couldn't remember the last time he went in there so it should be safe, for now at least. I left Rich propping up the thingy and nipped inside to get the keys. When I returned, he was looking at the item with a questioning face.

"So how did you actually make this, then?" he asked.

"Erm, well, bits of Lego and…"

"Well, it doesn't look like Lego. Are you *sure* this is yours? I don't want Mr Potter to come back and say that you've stolen it while he's been off at his alien convention whatnot. Looks like another of Mr Potter's garden decorations if you ask me."

Rich was right. The thing from the pond did look well suited to the decorations in Mr Potter's garden. But there was something about it that made me certain it was linked to the hamsters in some way. I needed to get a closer look at it, but my story was starting to unravel.

"Umm. Err. Erm," I mumbled.

"Your story is starting to unravel, laddo. I'm not helping you move this any further until you actually tell me what this is."

Not sure what to do, I stepped towards it. I ran my hand over its surface, hoping for a handle or a button or, at the very least, a flash of inspiration. Thankfully, my fingers touched on a small notch. I hooked under it and pulled, closing my eyes tight, not knowing what I would find.

The central section of the – whatever it was – opened and flopped down, suspended by some kind of hinge.

"Well, OK then," said Rich, staring at the newly opened flap and nodding.

I followed his eyeline and gasped.

On the interior of the flap, hanging upside down, was a picture. It was crudely drawn on something a bit papery and it was me! Me, clearly recognizable by my brown curly hair. Me, wearing a vest that had an O drawn on it. Me, surrounded by furry golden blobs worshipping at my feet.

"OK, then.

That's quite a ... creative school project. Sure different from the projects we did back in my day."

I laughed nervously, not quite believing what I'd seen myself. At least Rich seemed satisfied that the thingy was mine. Hundreds of questions were thundering in my brain. I tried to block them out as Rich finished helping me get it into the shed. I locked up and ran back into my house, hoping that would give Rich the message to leave. I could hear him mutter "But how did it turn the water red" as I shut the back door behind me. Just then, Dad's boxy blue car pulled into our drive.

***

For the rest of the day, I couldn't think about anything except what was in the shed. The more I thought about the strange object, the more convinced I was that it was some kind of spaceship. This threw up many more questions. Where exactly did the hamsters come from if they came from space? Did this make them alien hamsters? And how on earth did they have a picture of me? Against all odds, and while certainly making NO SENSE AT ALL, the evidence seemed to be pointing to my devoted group of hamsters being ALIEN HAMSTERS. Was I the first human to make contact with aliens? Aliens that I'd just sent away? Oh no!

That night, when all was quiet, I tiptoed out to Dad's shed. I didn't want to switch on the light so I had brought my torch and, in its dim light, I could see the picture of my face grinning out benevolently at the audience of adoring hamsters. Creepy! I investigated the cavity that the flap had covered – it seemed to contain an intricate network of wires and tunnels. I pulled at other parts of the ship's (for I was now CONVINCED it was a ship) outer shell until a small part, about the size of a pencil sharpener, snapped off in my hand. Ooops. If this was indeed the hamsters' ship, I should probably try not to break it.

All that gesticulating from Tibbles made sense now. The hamsters had needed my help to get their ship out of the pond. That's why they'd sought me out. The explanation almost made sense, except why did they have a picture of me? I couldn't wait to see what Stan thought of all this.

How had I got it so badly wrong? I had been so focused on what the hamsters could do for me. After all, they treated me like their god. I thought they were there to serve me. Instead, I should have been asking what they needed me to do *for them*. I had been a terrible god.

From Fluffy the 1000th, the Great and Most Fluffisome,

Tender-Hearted Leader of Hamsters

To Tibbles, Servant

Date HCT 172,479

Servant,

The spaceship's signal has resumed its transmission. However, it is still not functioning correctly as I am unable to control it remotely. The success of this mission still hangs in the balance, so I am sending down my bodyguards to help *finish* the mission.

F

CHAPTER FIFTEEN

On Monday, I had wanted to arrive at school nice and early, ready to shock Stan with my news – there are just some things you can't explain over the phone – but Martha had insisted on dressing herself for nursery, which made everything late. Dad didn't even have time to kiss me goodbye as I rushed into school, annoyed that I'd have to wait until break to speak to Stan. But something strange appeared to be going on around the building. Teachers and support staff kept appearing at the classroom door, asking if

Miss Harper had noticed anything. In the corridor, I actually saw Mrs Scout, the Head, crawling on her hands and knees. When she saw me looking, she jumped up, smoothed down her skirt and popped her head around the classroom door.

"Be alert, Helen. I'm going to have to call someone in," she said before disappearing down the corridor.

Just five minutes later, a message flashed up on the class whiteboard, which read "All pupils and staff: pack up your bags and file out into the playground."

As we walked into the playground, I could see a huge van, with the words BLACK CAT PEST SERVICES on the side, parked out the front.

"What's going on?" I asked Miss Harper, who looked a bit surprised that I had willingly spoken to her.

"Sounds like there's some kind of infestation at school," she replied. "Mice or rats or something. This guy is assessing the situation before we're let back in. It shouldn't be long."

This was a terrible development. Surely the presence of an exterminator could only mean one thing: the hamsters had moved out of my house and into the school!

Hoping Miss Harper wouldn't notice, I dragged Stan round the corner where we shouldn't be overheard. Then I explained everything, from me sending the hamsters away, to the spaceship and the exterminator.

"That's a lot of information to take in at nine forty-seven on a Monday morning.

Wow!" admitted Stan.

"But – space hamsters, Stan! Hamsters – from space!"

"Yes, I heard you."

"And so did I," came a voice from around the corner. "Wow, Olly. You don't say much and then what you do say is completely loony-tunes – out-of-this-world wackadoodle."

Oh, bum.

"I don't know what you *think* you heard, Hugh," I started, trying to sound authoritative and convincing and feeling neither. "Stan and I were just practising our lines for our – um – performance at the Leavers' Party on Friday."

Hugh laughed. "You? Onstage? How come, as the chief organizer for the party, I don't know anything about this?"

"Well, that was because we wanted

to make sure it was good before we told anyone," I retorted, desperately trying to throw him off the scent.

"It sounds brilliant," said Hugh.

"What? Really?"

"I would pay money to see you, the silent but deadly Olly, up onstage. You couldn't do it even if your life depended on it," Hugh said. "I'll put you down for it right now. What's it called?"

"Masters of the Hamsterverse," interjected Stan with a bit TOO much enthusiasm.

Oh boy!

***

As it turned out, removing a colony of space hamsters from a school is quite a time-consuming job (not that anyone else knew they were space hamsters). Gerald, the man from Black Cat Pest Services, whose cat was prowling around the playground, would not be hurried and Mrs Scout decided to close the school for the day. We all milled around the playground as teachers called parents and made arrangements. Miss Harper handed me the phone to speak to Dad at work.

"I'm swamped here, Olly," Dad said. "The NSO has been inundated with reports of UFOs recently, and I'm having to double-check our records over the last few weeks. Such a pain. Can Stan keep you company?"

This was, to be honest, the best possible outcome – and I suspected I had Mr Potter to thank for all the calls to the National Space Observatory – as it gave me and Stan the opportunity to investigate the hamster ship more without Dad being around. We even got to travel on the school bus, that had been called back. As we were driven away from school, I glanced back at the large van parked outside and hoped that if my hamsters were super-intelligent enough to make a spaceship, they were clever enough to avoid being caught by an exterminator or his cat.

***

Stan gave a low whistle when he stepped into Dad's shed. We examined the spaceship in silence. I opened the central section again, to show the portrait of me, but this time something bothered me about it.

"It just doesn't look quite right," I said.

"Nonsense. They've caught your bouncy hair and your teeth perfectly. Yes, it's a bit basic but I'm not sure we can criticize hamster drawing skills," Stan responded. He considered the picture again for a few seconds. "I guess you don't tend to stand up that confidently. You really should. It's so much better for your posture!"

That was it! That's what had been bugging me. It *looked* like me but there was something different about the way I was standing. I looked proud and self-assured. Maybe the hamsters had just wanted me to look more god-like in the image?

Leaving the picture, Stan and I tried to find other openings in the spaceship, but I was aware that our great galumphing human fingers were at risk of breaking its delicate pieces. We needed to proceed with extreme caution. Really, what I needed was the hamsters, but I had no idea how to get them back from school, especially with Gerald and his cat sniffing around. And then there was the issue of the spaceship itself – there, in Dad's shed that he was really odd about anyone else going into. And now I'd put a hamster spaceship inside it! That wasn't going to go down well, although I couldn't tell which would be worse – Dad discovering I'd been in his shed, or Dad finding out about the hundreds of hamsters. I did not want to find out!

I'd *never* been allowed in Dad's special shed, which had led me to believe that it was full of dangerous heavy machinery. What was surprising and strange about the shed was that it was largely empty (not including the hamster spaceship) except for a chair, a desk and, propped in the corner under a grotty grey sheet, a rather fancy-looking telescope. In the desk were various bits of boring paperwork from Dad's childhood, including school reports, diaries and his Scarphall Secondary School 1997 Yearbook.

I thumbed through a selection of the school reports, finding those from primary school.

"*Ozzy is simply outstanding at science. I have no doubt he will achieve great things in his future,*" I read out to Stan.

"Looks like your dad was voted 'Biggest Boffin' and 'Most Likely to Bring About the Apocalypse' at the end of secondary school," replied Stan, who was flicking through Dad's yearbook, a photo falling out from between pages as he browsed. "Ha! Look at this!"

Stan turned the book to me and there was a photo of sixteen-year-old Dad – Ozzy Brown – complete with spots, braces on his teeth and so much curly hair, with such a severe central parting, it was like he was being attacked by a very lumpy pair of curtains. I made a mental note to avoid that hairdo in the future. I glanced over the page. Various friends had scribbled their "good luck for

the future" and "keep in touch" messages, making me realize that, in addition to being better at everything than me, he was also far more popular.

Then I noticed the fallen picture on the floor. It was tucked face-down under a large parcel wedged under the desk, shrouded in black. I pulled at the parcel, surprised at how light it was for its size. The black cover slipped away, revealing – a hamster cage! I couldn't believe it. I dropped down to my knees and looked at the pristine cage. It clearly wasn't new but had been parcelled away lovingly, with plastic tunnel segments stacked along one end, two hamster wheels (one yellow, one green) laid on their sides and two water bottles, one labelled "Fluffy" and the other "Scruffy". Even though there was a hamster spaceship in the shed, this cage seemed like an even stranger discovery. My mind raced.

"Let me see!" Stan's voice brought me back to the real world.

"This … cage. It's, like, the Rolls-Royce

of hamster cages. What's it doing here?"

I tried to pull it out further, to show it to Stan, and the movement wobbled the water bottles, revealing a hand-drawn note underneath, which read "RIP Fluffy and Scruffy". This was getting even stranger. Had this belonged to Dad?

Stan grabbed the face-down photo. I'd been so distracted by the cage, I'd forgotten to pick it up. As Stan turned the photo over, I suddenly knew why the hamster-drawn picture from the spaceship looked so like me but, also, *not* like me. It wasn't a picture of me. It was a picture of Dad! O for Ozzy!

ALIEN
CONSPIRACY
CHAT

> Chatroom for Alien Contact

WeAreNotAlone65: If anyone needs their pond draining, I can highly recommend Rich at PondULike.co.uk – best money I ever spent. Not only am I back to picking up signals, I'm certain I've nearly got enough evidence to be taken seriously this time.

Alien Con XXV was out-of-this-world amazing. Just what I needed to encourage me with my endeavours. By the time the next convention comes around, my name will be known nationally, internationally and, even, universally. Even you disbelievers out there will have to admit that aliens do exist.

ScarySpice222: Click on <u>this link</u> for all your alien needs

PartKlingon99: I wish you luck but do heed my warnings. As soon as you put your head above the parapet, you will be at risk. My memories are hazy but they're starting to come back to me. There was a time when I wasn't even sure who I was any more. I wish I

CHAPTER SIXTEEN

Have you ever needed to have an important conversation with your parents, but you're fairly sure it's not going to go well? You know the kind – where you have to admit to being in trouble at school, or you have to own up to accidentally smashing their favourite vase? Or perhaps you've had to tell them you've been hiding a colony of space hamsters in your house while they treated you as their god, but that they were now banished to school, being threatened by an exterminator and you've hidden their spaceship in the forbidden shed, and in doing so you realized that the hamsters had mistaken you for your dad, who, for some reason, is their *real* god? No?

After the discovery of the photo of Dad, not to mention the hamster cage, Stan and I discussed what I should do. I was fairly certain that Dad's weirdness about hamsters must somehow be related to everything, especially as I was now convinced the hamsters' picture in their spaceship was of Dad. My plan was to get Dad down to his shed when he came in from work and he would see the spaceship from Mr Potter's pond, and then I could explain everything. I'd hoped Stan would stay around for moral support, but his mum picked him up before Dad got home.

"Dad," I started as soon as he opened the back door, "there's been some weird things going on over the last few weeks that

I'd like to talk to you about."

This felt like a strong start: I had Dad's attention. He nodded encouragingly, so I continued.

"Erm. It's to do with some hamsters. And something in your shed."

I should not have mentioned the H word. Or the S word.

"In my shed?" Dad's face went pale. "You have been told NEVER to go in there. And you want to talk to me about *hamsters*? Oh, I'm sure this is a big joke to you. If you've been snooping around in my shed, I know exactly what you've found!"

"No, that's not what I wanted to—"

"I was going to show you at some point, but in my own time. You had no right to go in there." His voice was weirdly quiet. "My experience – my grief – nearly led to me giving up science."

"No, Dad. You don't understand. I mean, yes, I've been in your shed, but there's something you need to see."

"I don't need to see anything in there and I don't have time for this nonsense – I need to pick up Martha. Now, give me my keys. I should never have left them lying about. Really, Olly, I thought I could trust you."

I'd never seen Dad so angry. He grabbed the shed key out of my open palm and snatched his car keys from the kitchen counter. I sensed he almost slammed the door shut but, knowing the dangers of a slammed door, he had second thoughts and pulled it gently, but pointedly, closed behind him.

I felt horrible – there was a heaviness in my stomach, like I'd eaten a sack of rocks. Dad was furious at me but, worse than that,

I had failed to get him on side to help me with the space hamsters. That night, after an awkwardly silent dinner, I couldn't sleep. My best hope was that Tibbles and the other hamsters were clever enough to avoid the exterminator. I kept thinking that, if they realized what danger they were in at school, they'd come back to me. I wished I was brave enough to sneak out in the middle of the night to help them but, even if I was, there was no way I could get to Burton village. Hearing the sounds of everyone sleeping, I snuck downstairs. It was so quiet without the hamsters. I unlocked the back door and sat on the step. The sky was still fairly light, and I looked over at Martha's locked sandpit, remembering how much fun the hamsters had had in there – swimming, diving and burrowing.

As I looked at the sandpit, I noticed a

dark shadow underneath it – darker than any other shadow in the garden. I pushed myself off the step and went to look. It wasn't a shadow – it was a hole. It seemed odd that my safety-obsessed dad would place a sandpit over a *hole*. I knelt down and tried to push against the pearly pink plastic shell, hoping its smooth bottom would slide easily across the ground. It wasn't budging. I made toe-holes in the grass, locked my legs and heaved my weight against the sandpit, like a one-boy rugby scrum. I could feel it start to move. I pushed more, then had to stop abruptly, as I nearly fell into the large dark hole that the sandpit had been covering.

I grabbed a torch from the kitchen and shone it into the partly-uncovered hole. Even considering that I had recently found a hamster spaceship in my neighbour's pond, what I saw took me by surprise. The sandpit had been covering an underground cavern. I knew hamsters were good at digging, but the carefully constructed space was breathtaking. The space had different levels, like theatre seats, surrounding a stage or some kind of platform. And there, in pride of place, were my missing purple unicorn

rubber, my pencil sharpener, the Pokémon sock, Minecraft nail clippers and my Lego key ring, and, draped behind all of these, like a curtain backdrop, were my (rather muddy) favourite underpants! This must have been where the hamsters had been living. And not just living. This was where they had been worshipping me! Their rubbish, fake god.

I peered further and noticed holes at various points around the outside of the cavern, no doubt for a network of tunnels. I leant forward to try to move some mud and get a better look but the ground beneath me gave way and I ended up face down in my muddy pants. I had destroyed all the hamsters' work – their tunnels, their cavern, their weird Olly shrine. All I'd left was a muddy mess. I really was a terrible god.

***

The next morning, Dad still wasn't talking to me. Martha seemed to sense the mood and was, for once, kind. She gave me a cookie (well, a half-eaten one) and patted my hand before Dad drove her off to nursery. He didn't need to tell me he wasn't giving me a lift. His silent rage said it all. I should have been excited about getting the school bus again, but I felt horribly guilty about how I'd made Dad feel. Great – the trust and independence I'd hoped for was now feeling like a punishment. My Crunchy Golden Nobbles tasted like cardboard once again. As I battled to get them down past the lump in my throat, Stan called.

"Have you heard that school is closed again? Mum's received a message to say that the exterminator didn't catch the pests yesterday, so school's going to be fumigated."

I coughed and spluttered as one

stubborn nobble caught firmly in my throat. I was relieved to hear that the hamsters had avoided being caught by the exterminator – but *fumigation*? This was a million times worse.

"No school! Whoop whoop," I could hear Stan saying, while I tried to clear my throat and stop my eyes from watering.

"Not whoop whoop," I managed to wheeze. "*Fumigated*, Stan. That means they're going to, like, POISON my hamsters. Tibbles and the rest were clever enough to avoid being caught by the man and his cat, but they won't survive poison, will they? And, even if they do – what about Sharon?"

I slammed the phone down and tried to focus on what I needed to do. Somehow, I needed to get to school and save the hamsters!

From:	HPotter@wearenotalone.co.uk
To:	Newsdesk@scarphallspectator.org.uk
Date:	July 18th, 05:32
Subject:	AMAZING DISCOVERY! With proof!

Dear Sir/Madam,

I will be calling in today with some information
you will be very interested to see. I suggest you
reserve your front page for this piece of news. I
cannot risk saying anything more, but I will be at
your offices bright and early this morning.

Faithfully,

Mr H.M. Potter (retired)

CHAPTER SEVENTEEN

After running around like a headless chicken for a couple of minutes, achieving precisely nothing, I stopped, calmed down and forced myself to focus. With no Dad lift and no school buses running because the school was shut, my only choice was the local bus. I grabbed a couple of pounds of leftover birthday money then grabbed a paper straw from the kitchen cupboard and went upstairs to retrieve something. A vague plan was starting to form in my mind. Waiting for the bus, I felt horribly nervous. In my mind, I kept repeating what I needed to say to the driver in order to get a ticket. When the bus came, the driver smiled at me.

"Return ticket to Burton, please," I managed to mumble.

"Four pounds please."

What! How much?

"I … I'm afraid I don't have enough. I thought it would be £2, tops, for a child ticket."

"Well, you didn't ask for a child ticket. I've put it through as an adult ticket."

"Oh, I-I'm only eleven." He stared at me blankly. I reminded myself why I was catching the bus in the first place and forced myself to continue. I needed to take this bus. "So, a *child's* return ticket to Burton, please."

"No can do – once I've put it through, it needs paying or it comes out of my wages."

I stared at the driver, my heart pounding.

This was possibly the worst interaction ever with an adult. I had to get to school to save the space hamsters and the bus driver was trying to sell me an adult ticket. Did he think I looked eighteen?

"No worries, driver," said a nasal voice behind me. "I'll buy that one and young Olly here can buy a child's one."

I never expected my saviour to come in the shape of Mr Potter but, for once, I was glad to see him. He was wearing a new T-shirt, emblazoned with purple zigzag writing, screaming "Alien Con XXV", with floating silver alien heads creating a pattern on the white background. It was not tasteful and, for a second, I wondered whether Mr Potter and Miss Harper would get along. I hadn't seen Mr Potter since his pond had been drained and I'd been dreading a discussion with him in case the Pond-U-Like guy had mentioned his rather unusual discovery. It seemed rude not to sit with him after he'd helped me out. Thankfully, Mr Potter seemed far more interested in talking *at* me about the Alien Convention he'd attended.

"Ah, Olly, it was wonderful! I really hope your dad will open his mind to the idea of alien life-forms because there is a beautiful endlessness of possibilities out there."

I made vague noises in response because,

well, I feared that anything I said could give away my internal panic about the space hamsters. Thankfully, being used to my quietness, Mr Potter saw nothing unusual in my tentative nods and hmms. I zoned out from what he was saying to try and come up with an excuse for being at school – it was likely that'd I'd bump into a teacher or something and I needed to be ready.

"... so I'm heading there now, complete with all this evidence of alien activity. They HAVE to take me seriously this time." I tuned back into Mr Potter's monologue. What had he been talking about?

"They?"

"The newspapers. I'm heading there first, before I contact the Government Agency for Intergalactic Life-forms."

"The what?" I asked.

"I'm not surprised you've never heard of

it, the Government Agency for Intergalactic Life-forms? GAIL? It's *very* secret. But for those in the know." Mr Potter tapped the side of his nose a couple of times. "I'm convinced there is alien activity taking place RIGHT NOW in this area and I, Harold Potter, will become famous the world over for being the first human to accurately report and provide evidence of aliens. Just imagine! Finally, the name Harold Potter will *mean* something on this planet."

In spite of my nerves, I couldn't help giving a little snigger. I hadn't known Mr Potter's first name and I wondered whether I should mention to Mr Potter that his name is already massively famous, but just then, on the pavement, I saw Stan waving at me.

"Friend. Thanks. Bye," was all I managed to say to Mr Potter as I jumped up and rang the bell.

As I was getting off the bus, a thought flashed in my mind. Mr Potter wasn't potty at all – actually, he was getting quite close to the truth. And if he was at the point of telling other people about his discoveries, that put my hamsters in even more danger. Once they were safe from the exterminator, I *had* to help them get home.

"Stan!" I cried with relief as he hurried over. "What are you doing here?"

"Well, I figured you'd be on your way to help these hamsters and you might need a hand."

The school was shrouded in a blue plastic wrapping – like a tent had landed over the entire building. In Year 4 we did a project on the artist Christo, whose work involved wrapping things – I don't mean like birthday presents. He wrapped buildings and bridges. During our project, we wrapped small objects in toilet roll. It did not quite have the same effect. But now I see Christo was just ripping off his idea from what exterminators have to do to fumigate buildings, so I'm even less impressed!

We could see Gerald's van parked on the zigzag lines outside school. Gerald was leaning against it drinking from a thermos and wearing a grey polo shirt that had "Ask me about our PEST OF THE MONTH!" written on it. Phew, he hadn't started yet.

"How are we going to play this?" asked Stan.

"I need to get in and try to communicate with Tibbles," I said urgently. "We have to get the hamsters out somehow. They need to know how much danger they're in. And Tibbles needs to know that I've found the spaceship. Maybe I can actually help them get home."

"But how exactly are you going to do that?"

"No time for that! Can you try and distract Gerald for as long as possible to buy me some time? Just keep a lookout and send a warning if he's coming."

I hadn't told Stan about my plan. Something told me he wouldn't approve.

I found an opening in the plastic wrapping and slid between it and the school walls. The plastic material created a strange blue light which gave everything an eerie, otherworldly feeling. I located the main door and slipped in.

My first priority was to find Sharon, but as I headed to Hamster Class, I nipped into every classroom on the way, switching on computers and whiteboards. I was certain that no one, not even Miss Harper, would have given a thought to our class pet in the hurry to sort out the school. Sure enough, there Sharon was, in the classroom, sleeping away, unaware of the imminent danger. Beside her cage were a few pre-nibbled seed casings – evidence of Tibbles's presence and his continued adoration. Where could he and the other hamsters be?

Sitting at Miss Harper's desk, I quickly typed:

DANGER! GET OUT OF SCHOOL OR YOU WILL BE POISONED.

I'M SORRY FOR SENDING YOU AWAY. PLEASE RETURN.

I HAVE FOUND YOUR SHIP AND CAN HELP.

O

I pressed "Share to Whiteboard Network" – hopefully, wherever Tibbles and the others were hiding, they would see this message.

I took Sharon to the main entrance and left her there while I returned to my class's lockers. I took out the paper straw from my pocket and the handful of hamster poos I'd retrieved from my dressing gown. (Yes – I had failed to empty my dressing gown pocket of hamster poos for several days. Please don't judge me.) It was fiddly work trying to get the poos into the straw, but I didn't mind scattering some of them on the ground – it was part of the plan! I finally placed the poo-filled straw between two of the vents in Hugh's locker and, careful to blow rather than suck, I emptied the straw's contents into it.

There wasn't really anything more I could do. I returned to Sharon's cage, picked it up, went through the main entrance and walked straight into Gerald. Stan stood behind him, waving his arms and pointing.

"That's a great warning, thanks, Stan," I muttered.

"What do you think you're doing in there?" Gerald exploded. "I'm about to bombard this place with poison. No one – especially not a child – is supposed to be here at all. And I suppose your friend here was part of this prank?"

"It turns out the 'Pest of the Month' is schoolchildren," Stan piped up from behind, which did not help.

"Sir…" I stammered. He really was very angry. But then I remembered I had an important job. A position of trust. "I am my class's hamster monitor and I could not let our beloved Sharon become one of your many victims."

Stan looked as surprised as Gerald that I'd spoken with such force.

Now for the next part of my plan.

"Actually, sir, when I was in the school, I did notice something that I think you should see."

I led Gerald along the corridor to Hugh's locker. I pointed to the poos on the floor.

"There seem to be an awful lot of these round here."

"Interesting," he said. He knelt down and picked up a single hamster poo, squeezing, sniffing it and crumbling it between his fingers. "I can't believe I missed this. Do you know who this locker belongs to?"

"Hugh Botham," I said. "His dad owns Botham Buys Best here in Burton."

"A shop? A FOOD shop? Oh, deary me. This could be a public health DISASTER!" exclaimed the exterminator, and he rushed out to his van.

Stan was frowning at me. But I had space hamsters to save and, judging by the speed at which Gerald's van tore off down the street, I maybe had done that. Still worried for Sharon's safety, and assuming I couldn't sink much lower in Dad's estimation, there was nothing much I could do but return home and take Sharon with me. Out of nowhere, it dawned on me that I was about to achieve one of my end-of-year targets. A lot had happened since I'd written my target about getting to look after Sharon at my home. In all the ways I'd dreamt about making it happen, protecting our class hamster from an exterminator on the hunt for a colony of space hamsters was not one I'd imagined.

From Tibbles, Mission Lead for the Faithful on Operation O

To Fluffy the 1000th, the Great and Most Fluffisome,
Tender-Hearted Leader of Hamsters

Date HCT 172,482

Most Tender-Hearted Leader,

We have received a SIGN from Him. All is forgiven! And what we all prayed for so arduously – the Miracle of the Spaceship Retrieval – has come to pass. I *knew* our faith would be rewarded.

We have no need for extra help. There is no need to send your bodyguards. You, our Most Fluffisome, should not be left alone in orbit at this time. Although I am certain that O, in his kindness and wisdom, will also find a way to give you what you deserve.

Your servant,

Tibbles

CHAPTER EIGHTEEN

I'd hoped to hide Sharon in my room for a bit while I worked out the best time to tell Dad about her. Sadly, that was not possible because as I put my key in the door it was opened from the inside.

"They were going to fumigate the school and I had to save Sharon and I couldn't think where to…" The words tumbled out of me, but Dad put his hand up.

"I looked in the shed," he said. "What on earth have you put in there?"

Ah.

I left Sharon in her cage on the kitchen counter as we headed out into the garden. I pointed out the muddy mess still visible under Martha's sandpit as we walked to the shed. Over the next few minutes, I explained everything that had happened, from meeting Tibbles in the first place, to my nightly entertainment for all the hamsters. I explained about finding the spaceship in Mr Potter's pond and the hamster tunnels under the sandpit. Virtually everything I said sounded completely ridiculous, but the evidence existed – Dad couldn't deny that.

"They'd built a shrine to me and treated me like their god," I said as I finished my explanation. "But I think they were mistaken. I think they came here searching for you. Look."

We'd entered his shed and I opened the central section of the spaceship, revealing the picture of him as a kid. Dad dropped down into the chair like a sack of overwhelmed potatoes – I guess it was rather a lot of information to take in. He sat there in silence, staring at the image of himself surrounded by adoring hamsters. Seconds turned into minutes and he still hadn't spoken.

"Dad? Who were Fluffy and Scruffy?"

For a few more minutes, the silence continued – for so long, in fact, that I started to doubt whether I'd actually asked my question. Then suddenly Dad looked at me and cleared his throat.

"I've never told you this but, around your age, I had two hamsters – Fluffy and Scruffy. I adored those furry little scamps!"

Dad? Notorious hater of hamsters? Actually *owned* hamsters?

"I spent every evening playing with them, telling them about my day, feeding them, letting them run around in tunnels I created for them. Tunnels just out there." Dad pointed out into the garden and I remembered that our house was actually the house *he* grew up in too.

"Towards the end of Year 6, I got a bit distracted. I was totally focused on my project for the science fair. Being regarded as a bit of a genius meant everyone was expecting great things from me and I didn't want to let them down. Actually, I didn't want to let myself down."

I'd never really thought about it this way. The pressure people like Dad must be under to keep succeeding. For once, I was quite glad not to be a mega-genius.

Dad continued his story. "Through endless observations and research, I'd realized that the most likely way of making contact with aliens was if I could send something through a black hole. I made a space capsule and filled it with various things for an alien species to find – an English dictionary, a pocket atlas, my scientific calculator, a copy of my favourite science-fiction book, *Primordial Soup, Space Goggles and You* by Marjorie Morley, a packet of Fruit Polos and a photo of myself. As I was obsessing over the space capsule and the necessary calculations to fire it into space at exactly

the right time – so it would shoot past space detritus, spinning satellites and orbiting planets, and enter a black hole at the edge of our universe – my poor, beloved hamsters were pining for me."

"But," I interrupted, "your science fair space capsule? That's still at school! You never fired it!"

"Oh, that one was just a spare – something to show at school. I had done all my calculations based on launching the capsule from this garden. Oh, how I wish I'd decided to launch from the school playground. There's not a day that's gone past for the last thirty years when I haven't regretted that decision."

"Why? I don't understand."

"Once it was launched, I wanted to track the capsule's progress with my super-powerful GalileoX2000 telescope there."

Dad gestured to the telescope under the sheet in the corner. "I was going to watch my space capsule while cuddling Fluffy and Scruffy. But when I went to their cage after launching the capsule, the door was open and the cage was empty. I noticed a trail of their bedding leading out from the cage to – well, to the launch site. The now crisp and burnt launch site."

Dad let out a sob.

"If only I'd arranged for the launch to happen at school." Sob. "Then Fluffy and Scruffy would have survived." Sob. "As it was, they must have bedded down under the space capsule in the garden and I..." Another sob. "INCINERATED THEM!"

Tears were rolling freely down Dad's face now and I didn't really know what to do. I'd never seen him like this. I hugged him until his sobs slowed down and he took deep breaths into my now-wet neck.

"Can you see why I didn't want anything to do with hamsters, ever again?"

As Dad had been recounting his tale, my mind had been racing. Everything was starting to fit into place.

"I don't think you *did* incinerate Fluffy and Scruffy," I said. "What if they climbed *inside* your space capsule? Instead of killing them, you sent them off on a great adventure and – clearly – they survived. Not only did they survive, they created a colony of hamsters that *somehow* were clever enough to develop their own society. Their own technology. Their own religion! No wonder they worship you as their god!"

"I suppose…" Dad started.

"There's no suppose about it," I said. "Although I don't quite get how the hamsters became super intelligent or how they achieved all this in thirty years."

"Well, thirty years is a long time for hamsters. It's widely accepted that nine human days is the same as a hamster year, so by that calculation..." Dad mumbled some numbers under his breath, "just over one thousand, two hundred and sixteen hamster years have passed. Imagine human development over that amount of time. And who knows how the black hole affected the hamsters. Perhaps your theory is possible. After all, the mixture of fermions, bosons, quarks and—"

"Fantastic," I interrupted, keen to distract Dad from the scientific gobbledegook. I pulled Dad to his feet. "We now need to save your colony of space hamsters and get them back where they came from."

We stepped out of the shed and my

heart leapt as I spotted Tibbles and his black box plus three other hamsters scampering towards us.

"It's Tibbles!" I cried, punching the air. "He saw my messages at school. This is amazing."

But as the hamsters stopped in front of us, I noticed there was something odd about Tibbles. His black eyes were trained on me, but gone was the look of adoration.

"Tibbles?" I asked tentatively. "I'm sorry, I..."

He interrupted, chattering away and, from his black box, instead of the usual "Tibbles, Tibbles, Tibbles", I heard:

"Be warned, you traitorous and false god known as O. We are here to succeed where others have failed. In the name of Fluffy the 1000th, the Great and Most Fluffisome, our Tender-Hearted Leader, we demand you take us to the spaceship, or we will destroy you, right here, right now."

CHAPTER NINETEEN

Being attacked by four hamsters was not particularly scary, even though they were very determined and bitey. Their flying kicks, punches and scratches were fairly unpleasant, but the hamsters were only targeting our shins and ankles, so Dad and I overpowered them with ease. We managed to grab two hamsters each and headed into the house, where we wrestled them into the cage with a sleeping Sharon. The presence of the massive earth hamster seemed to calm them, and they stared out at us from between the cage bars, only occasionally reaching their paws out of the cage and hissing in what they probably hoped was a menacing way but which was, actually, still really cute.

"Poor little hamsters. They must be hungry," said Dad, who grabbed an apple and started chopping it.

Tibbles chattered and hissed back at dad with an intense and angry look.

"You will not distract us from our solemn mission with bribes, you wrinkled lackey of a fake idol," translated the black box.

So the black box *was* a communications device. These space hamsters were remarkable. If only Tibbles's black box had been working properly the whole time – we could have avoided so many problems.

"I'm sorry you're upset, Tibbles, we just want to help," I said gently.

"I am Honey Cheeks, chief bodyguard and hench-hamster to Fluffy the 1000th. I care not about the traitor Tibbles and the other faithful. Their job on the planet was to locate you, their supposed god, O – the god described in our stories passed down from the Ancient Ones – and then they were going to…"

Honey Cheeks stopped speaking as Dad sprinkled pieces of apple into the cage. I think all the revelations over the last few minutes had caused Dad to have some kind of brain fart – and all he seemed able to do was basic tasks. Honey Cheeks paused to pick up a chunk, and I took the opportunity to look at her more closely. (Honey Cheeks sounded to me like a name for a girl hamster, but I wasn't about to get closer to find out. She was quite intimidating for a tiny hamster.) From where I was standing, she looked identical to Tibbles, including the black box that had always marked Tibbles out as special. The only clear difference in looks was that she was looking very angry.

"I'm sorry, Honey Cheeks. You were saying…" I encouraged, feeling very strange about finally *conversing* with a hamster. "Who are the Ancient Ones you mentioned?"

Honey Cheeks waved the piece of apple around as she spoke. "The 'Ancient Ones' were Fluffy the First and Scruffy the Splendid. The founders of our colony."

I caught Dad's eye. This hamster was confirming what I had suggested only moments ago. Dad nodded blankly and started grating some cheese.

Honey Cheeks continued, "We are here to finish the job that Tibbles and the faithful were sent here to do."

"Didn't they come in peace? All they

seemed to want to do was praise O and collect a few souvenirs," I said.

"Ha! The 'great and powerful' O speaks but he is no god. He is a fool!" Honey Cheeks pointed her apple chunk at me accusingly. "And he is only worshipped by fools."

Clearly, these hamsters also recognized me from their picture of O but, this time, they were not fans. And even though I now knew it was really Dad who was O, it didn't feel like the best time to correct this.

"Under the tender-hearted leadership of Fluffy the 1000th, we have no need for other leaders – or gods. Fluffy the 1000th is our one true master, but Tibbles and the faithful have been most determined in holding on to their beliefs. They didn't even know for certain that O existed beyond the stories. Thanks to their faith, they could not accept the glorious rule of Fluffy the

1000th. So, instead, they were sent on this mission – not to find O, but to destroy him. And themselves in the process. Due to the unfortunate landing and the spaceship being submerged, the mission has not succeeded – yet. That is why we are here."

"What are you supposed to do?" I asked.

"Our mission is—" Honey Cheeks stopped as Dad rained cheese gratings down on her. She picked a piece off her sleek fur and held it with her free paw. "Our mission is to fix the spaceship so it can do the job it was intended for."

"Return the hamsters home?" I suggested hopefully.

"No, you feeble excuse for a deity. The spaceship has been designed to explode, taking the hamsters, O and most of this planet with it."

This was, to be honest, terrible news. Even though we'd trapped the evil hench-hamsters, finding out that our garden shed contained basically a bomb big enough to destroy Earth definitely put a downer on my day.

I found myself thinking about my third target, about making an impact on the school. This wasn't what I'd had in mind.

Dad's reaction was to grate some more cheese.

"But ... but ... but..." I tried desperately to reason with Honey Cheeks. "If you explode the spaceship, you yourselves will be killed."

"We have been trained to fight and serve. Our only duty is to Fluffy the 1000th and if he has decided that our fate is to die on this terrible planet, so be it. You have us trapped for now, but we WILL succeed eventually, and Earth will be destroyed. It shouldn't be too much of a loss. After all, what can this place possibly have that is worth saving?"

With that, Honey Cheeks bit triumphantly into the piece of apple.

Suddenly, the steely look in her black eyes softened and her entire body juddered. She made a cooing sound – a sound I'd never heard from any hamster.

The black box translator piped up. "Ooooh. That's good."

Honey Cheeks took another bite. The cooing got louder.

"My goodness. I've never tasted anything so..."

She stuffed some cheese in her mouth.

"That's even better. What if I..."

Then she got another piece of apple and another piece of cheese and shoved them into her mouth together. Cue mega-cooing.

"I can't believe this! The flavours! The sensations! The crispness of whatever this is. And the creaminess of this yellow stuff! I have never experienced food like it. It is a miracle!"

Suddenly, Honey Cheeks and her hench-hamsters were stuffing cheese and apple into their cheeks like their lives depended on it. Me and Dad stared at them, knowing OUR lives depended on it.

I cleared my throat. "Honey Cheeks?"

"Yes," said Honey Cheeks, trying to bow at me. "Oh, by bost wuh-hifful one. Wey hif ryong..."

I had no idea what Honey Cheeks was saying and asked her to speak more clearly. Reluctantly, she removed several chunks of apples from her cheeks.

"Oh, most worshipful one. We have wronged you greatly and yet you show us kindness – you and your wizened disciple – with this nectar of the gods."

Well, that was quite a turnabout.

"Actually, I am no god. I am Olly Brown and this is my dad, Ozzy." Dad stepped forward, gave a little bow and dropped a handful of pine nuts into the cage. "*He* is the person your Ancient Ones called O. Thirty years ago, his pet hamsters Fluffy and Scruffy *somehow* made it into space. That those hamsters survived, developed super intelligence and established a successful colony in space could *seem* like a miracle, but it was all an accident. 'O' is not someone who should be worshipped. He was just a heartbroken boy who loved his pets."

Honey Cheeks sat up on her back paws, then dropped to the floor, front paws outstretched.

"Only a true and noble god would say that. You are great indeed! Do you deny your own existence to test me? I am now a believer! What can we do to earn your forgiveness?"

Oh dear! This wasn't going quite how I expected. This hamster had gone from being on a death-mission to being a loyal convert in a matter of seconds.

"No!" I insisted. "You must listen. No one here is a god. No one needs to be worshipped and no one needs to be forgiven. But Tibbles and the faithful, as you call them, weren't entirely wrong in their beliefs, were they? Even without evidence, their faith led them here, to find the person who had loved and cared for their ancestors. So they were right in some ways, weren't they? Those hamsters do not deserve to die. If Fluffy the 1000th is intent on destroying those hamsters, our planet, and any threat to his leadership, *he* is the one who does not deserve your loyalty."

Honey Cheeks listened with her head to one side as the black box translated. When it finished, she threw herself on to the cage floor again, bowing down before me.

"You are wise indeed! What can we do?"

I thought quickly. "If you are able to show us how to prevent the spaceship exploding, you can spend the rest of your days experiencing all the food this planet has to offer."

Honey Cheeks found this a most agreeable suggestion and the hamsters allowed themselves to be lifted out of the cage by me and Dad, ready to go to the spaceship. Sharon slept on in the cage, unaware that we were about to try and save the world.

As we headed up the garden, Dad whispered, "Are you sure about this, Olly? Only minutes ago, these hamsters were going to destroy us all."

Thankfully, the hamster's black box didn't pick up Dad's concerns. I nodded at him. I had to trust that these hamsters were now on our side. We set them down on the floor of the shed and watched as they set to work, opening sections of the spaceship that I'd never realized existed. All four disappeared into the spaceship.

"Even if these hamsters blow us up – whether accidentally or on purpose," said Dad while we waited, "I want you to know that I am proud of you, and I think you make a very good god of hamsters."

Honey Cheeks reappeared.

"There's good news and there's bad news, oh worshipful one," she said to me. "The bad news is that we don't seem able to disconnect the explosives, so they are still likely to destroy your planet."

Gulp. Dad went pale and flopped down on his chair.

"What's the good news?" I asked hopefully.

"The picture of you is really excellent, merciful O! Our artists did a great job, don't you think?"

I sighed. *That* was the good news?

"Can the spaceship still fly?" I asked.

"Can it fly with no one on it?"

"Yes," replied Honey Cheeks.

"So, let's just send it up into space and let it explode there, right?" I said.

It was the only plan we had, so it had to work. According to Honey Cheeks, all that was needed was to press two buttons: one to start the ten-minute countdown for the bomb, the second to start the engines, and the spaceship should just fly straight up.

By now, Dad was simply a curled-up ball in his chair, rocking himself gently. I knew he had worries about these hamsters' intentions. Asking them to press the buttons definitely felt like a leap of faith.

"OK!" I said. "Press those buttons."

The first button was pressed and an ominous ticking sound started up. At least it hadn't led to immediate destruction. I breathed a little easier. Now, all Honey Cheeks had to do was press the other button. She did. Nothing happened. Dad's rocking became more pronounced and he started gently humming to himself.

"What's going on?" I asked as seconds ticked away.

"The start-up button does not appear to be working. It might be something to do with the spaceship lying in water for so long. It seems jammed."

The hamsters were taking it in turns to fly at the button with precise and powerful kicks. However, their skills and considerable strength – for hamsters – were not enough.

"Move aside," I said, and jabbed at the button with all my might. The spaceship jumped into action, raising slightly off the floor and hovering for a couple of seconds. A grinding sound emanated from its centre, getting increasingly louder.

"The finger of power," cried Honey Cheeks. "Another miracle!"

I quickly snatched back my finger and the hamsters jumped down from the central console as the spaceship rose higher and higher. It broke through the shed roof with ease, rapidly rising into the sky until we could see the hamster-wheel-shaped ship no more.

Overwhelmed, Dad slid off his chair into a heap on the floor.

"Your servant has perhaps died," commented Honey Cheeks. "Can I offer my services in his place?"

I knew Dad wasn't dead – he was just in shock.

"You do not need to serve me – or anyone," I told her. "You have just saved the Earth and now you should be free to lead

your own lives. Why don't you go out there, find more delicious food? I have a feeling you'll enjoy blueberries."

"Yes, yes, our master. We will seek out these blueberries of which you speak, and we will spread the word of your glorious actions here today."

"No! That's not what I—"

But it was too late. Honey Cheeks and her fellow hench-hamsters scampered away, disappearing into the muddy mess below Martha's sandpit.

Dad started to rouse himself from the floor. "What happened?"

"The spaceship is heading up and the planet is safe, I think," I said.

Even though Dad had been fairly useless during the important saving-the-world situation that had just occurred, I still needed his help.

"Can you head to work and somehow remove any evidence of this UFO we've just sent up into space? It might be rather difficult to explain – and anyone tracing its path back to its source would know it had come from here. I'm not sure we want that kind of attention, do we?"

Dad nodded silently, and I decided that a cup of tea might get him back to his usual self.

I headed into the house and, while the kettle was boiling, I gently stroked the spotted back of the still-sleeping Sharon. Typical! She'd slept through all the action. She opened one eye, then the other, and saw the mess that the hench-hamsters had made in her usually tidy cage. She rose up on her hind legs and starting angrily chattering away.

It was only at that point that I realized

how useful it would have been to ask Honey
Cheeks for her black box translation device!

From Fluffy the 1000th, the Great and Most Fluffisome,

Tender-Hearted Leader of Hamsters

To Honey Cheeks, chief bodyguard and hench-hamster

Date HCT 172,482

Bodyguard,

Please send a report. What is going on? Why has nothing exploded yet?

Now my scanners are picking up an incoming missile – coming straight at the Mothership.

Impact in 10, 9, 8, 7...

Taking evasive action.

F

Beep

Beep

Beep

Beep

Beep

Beep ...

> Chatroom for Alien Contact

WeAreNotAlone65: I have just picked up an EXPLOSION in space. Not only that – some piece of space detritus appears to be heading straight for Earth. My devices cannot tell whether it is falling or flying. In all my years searching the skies, I have never experienced so much alien activity.

This excitement could be getting to me, however. As I was working in my garden, several yellowish rodents ran past me. Voles perhaps, or dormice? And I swear one of them was talking about blueberries. I'd best not mention this to the "you-know-who" agency. I think I've finally got them to start taking me seriously.

ArmchairAlienFan: What makes YOU so special? Posting on here. Thinking you're all that.

ScarySpice223: Click on this link for all your alien needs

PartKlingon99: Voles? Don't talk to me about voles! It's space hogs you need to be watching out for. Great big snuffly things with tusks and wiry hair. That's what

CHAPTER TWENTY

That evening, Tibbles and the rest of the hamsters returned to the house. They had seen my apology message at school and had returned hoping to find their spaceship and return to their colony. It turns out I didn't need a hamster translator to understand how sad Tibbles was when he saw the empty space in the shed and the hole in its roof, not to mention the destroyed O shrine under the sandpit.

After having put Martha to bed, Dad insisted on staying up to meet the hamsters.

Earlier he had returned from the NSO with great excitement, saying he'd arrived in time to witness the explosion of the hamster spaceship when it had collided with another Unidentified Flying Object. He couldn't be certain, but, according to what Honey Cheeks had told us about the mothership orbiting Earth, Dad was fairly confident that the now-destroyed UFO was, indeed, Fluffy the 1000th's ship.

The evil hamster had been hoping to witness the ultimate destruction of Tibbles's band of hamsters, not to mention our planet, and had been blown to smithereens himself instead. The hamsters and Earth were safe.

I watched Dad play with the hamsters downstairs as they scurried over every surface. He looked more carefree than I'd ever seen him. He didn't even seem bothered by the health and safety issues of hosting hundreds of hamsters. Not even by all the hamster poo!

Sharon lazily watched the celebrations from her cage, greedily eyeing the food that Dad kept appearing with. Tibbles, ever attentive, occasionally pushed food-based love tokens through the bars, where Sharon would gobble them with an ungrateful squeak. However, I couldn't leave Tibbles to his courtship entirely – there were serious things we needed to discuss. I wrote out YES and NO so he would be able to answer simple questions. I started by asking where in school the hamsters had been hiding. It took a few guesses but finally Tibbles answered YES to the ventilation pipes. I then explained our meeting with Honey Cheeks and the hench-hamsters. Tibbles clearly had no idea he'd been set up by Fluffy the 1000th. He read my messages with increasing alarm. When

I asked him if he still wished to return to the colony, he ran to YES. I asked him if he knew another way to get home, and this time he ran to NO.

Finally, I wrote down what I had been dreading telling Tibbles.

I AM NOT YOUR GOD.

Tibbles moved to the YES.

Before I wrote anything more, I pointed over to Dad, who, at that moment, was covered in hamsters from head to foot, making him look like he was wearing a lumpy, furry onesie. Tibbles shook his head and padded over to my still-outstretched finger, which he held in a tight hamster-hug.

He gazed up at me with such adoration that I didn't want to break his heart any further. He'd spent a lifetime believing in O. The least I could do was help him get home.

***

School returned to normal the next day, although how normal can things really be once you've saved the world from a megalomaniac space hamster? I couldn't wait to tell Stan everything that had happened the day before, but the blue tarpaulin that had been wrapped around the school building was now covering Botham Buys Best, and that was the only thing anyone was talking about. Hugh was nowhere to be seen.

"Hugh deserves lots of things but not this," Stan said to me at break, jumping in before I got a chance to start my tale of hench-hamsters and saving the world. I wasn't in the mood for a lecture.

"Well, your mum said the shop was expensive and rubbish," I countered. "It's not like the exterminator will actually *find* anything. Now the hamsters are back at mine, everything can return to normal."

Stan's brow creased. "Even when they don't find anything to exterminate, Botham Buys Best's reputation is ruined. I think that's really low. I'd hoped you working with Hugh on the party might have helped you two become friends. But instead, you completely stitched him up. And you can't behave like that without it coming back to bite you on the bum."

"So, that's why you nominated me for the party? It hasn't got anything to do with me and Hugh – it's because you want to get close to Amelia Fletcher!"

I stormed away from Stan, not having time to be bothered about Horrendous Hugh, or about Stan's schoolboy crush. I had actual *real* problems to deal with, like a colony of space hamsters with no way of returning home.

It turns out, Stan was more right than I could have imagined. During the next lesson, Miss Harper, in a fluffy rainbow cardigan, announced that Mr Botham had informed the school that Hugh would not be returning for the remainder of the term and he would no longer be providing free refreshments for the Leavers' Party. The entire class groaned. Even Miss Harper looked disappointed about the lack of fizzy ferret chews, but she jutted out her chin and made a further announcement to the class.

"Don't be disheartened," she said,

putting on her *everything will be fine* voice. "This is exactly why we have a second-in-command. The party will go ahead, on Friday, as planned – it's now the responsibility of Olly."

She started to clap and everyone – the entirety of the Hugh Botham Fan Club – slowly, reluctantly joined in. I caught Stan's eye, who shrugged in a very justified "I told you so" kind of way.

Karma is a pig.

***

I spent the rest of the day flitting between stewing over how to get the hamsters back to their colony and mulling over how to, in two days, prepare for a party everyone was now counting on me to organize. During the last half hour of the day, my mind whirred and failed to concentrate on the class book that Miss Harper was reading. I was getting even further away from completing my crocheted hamster.

After school, I waited for Dad as the other kids got on the bus. Dad was *never* late. Stan approached. Great. Another lecture.

"Look – you're right. I did volunteer you for the Leavers' Party to try and smooth things over with you and Hugh because, however much you may deny it, I think you'd actually like more friends," he said, largely to the back of my head. When I didn't respond, he continued, "Do you know what I wrote for one of my targets? To help *you* be more confident!"

I turned around. "And what about Amelia?"

Stan blushed and looked down at his shoes.

"I have no idea what you're talking about," he said. "But I'd like everyone to get along, which includes Hugh, so this does need to be made right. Promise me you'll do that, and I'll help you out. I'll be your second-in-command for the party."

I appreciated Stan's offer of help, but I wasn't suddenly filled with confidence that everything would turn out OK for the party, especially as I now had to add "apologize to Hugh" to my to-do list.

Just then, Dad came tearing around the corner, his awful boxy car almost tipping over on to two wheels. Could this *really* be my dad? Mr Safety Conscious?

"I've been doing some research," he panted, poking his head through the car window, his hair sticking up in curly lumps. "And I *think* I've located the black hole the hamsters need to go through. Oh, hello, Stan!"

It was a good job my friend knew what was going on, otherwise that would have been a very strange sentence to overhear.

"According to my calculations, I *think* the black hole will be accessible by some kind of projectile very soon."

"*Very soon*? You *think*? When can you be more certain?" I asked.

For a super space scientist, Dad was being super vague.

"It's not going to be easy," Dad continued. "I need to do some more calculations, based on the orbit of various planets, the trajectories of any comets or space detritus that could be crossing its path. It's not a simple calculation. So many variables – including that we have no idea what the hamsters will be travelling in. It's not like I can use an NSO device – or call up NASA and ask to borrow a rocket."

"But … you've done it before," I said.

"Yes, a long time ago with lots of time to prepare."

Stan piped up, "But you're the superstar scientist of our school. Everyone knows how good you are, Mr Brown. We see your Space Capsule 2 in our school hall every day."

OF COURSE!

"Dad! Was Space Capsule 2 a fully working model? Could we use that?" I asked.

"You're right! Goodness, is that still hanging there? I was happy to donate it to the school so that I would never be reminded of my hamster horror. Yes, as long as it hasn't been messed around with, it should be fine. I'll need to do more calculations and possibly some adjustments for weight, but that's probably our best chance."

Suddenly, things were looking up. We had a solution to the hamster spaceship issue and now there was the simple task of planning the Leavers' Party over two days. Easy!

Sadly, however, Stan was true to his word and even though Dad was kind enough to offer him a lift to our house for some party planning, Stan *insisted* that we made a stop on the way – at Botham Buys Best.

People walking by stopped and stared at the blue tarpaulin around the shop. Mr Botham was outside, shooing them away. Mr Botham was a large man, whose muscles bulged through his Botham Buys Best polo shirt. The Black Cat Pest Services van was parked outside, but there was no sign of Gerald or his cat.

I approached Mr Botham nervously, feeling like my collar was tightening around my neck. Up close, he loomed over me and all I could see was his blood-red shirt in front of my eyes. "Erm, is Hugh around?" I asked.

"Shop's closed and Hugh doesn't want to see anyone," Mr Botham huffed. "You from his class?"

"Yes, I'm Olly Brown – I just came to…"

"Olly Brown? I know you! You made Hugh's life a misery with your name calling in Year 3."

That definitely didn't sound like the true version of events. I was surprised that Hugh's family still remembered my unfortunate slip. But I'd spent years not having any friends because of that. Wasn't that punishment enough?

"Come to gloat at this mess?" Mr Botham continued, towering over me.

"No! No! I just wanted to check Hugh's OK. He will be missed at the end of term and especially at the party. He should come back to school. I know the whole pest control thing is just a misunderstanding but—"

"And what do *you* know about that?" interrupted Mr Botham.

"Nothing," I squeaked, almost reaching hamster pitch. I ran back to the safety of the car, calling over my shoulder, "Just tell Hugh that I came by to apologize."

There. Job done.

Stan didn't look convinced by my effort but, short of overpowering the shed-sized Mr Botham and fighting my way through the blue tarpaulin, I didn't think there was much more I could do.

Back at mine, Stan and I came up with party ideas, while Dad headed back to the observatory, keen to use the scientific equipment to do more calculations for the hamsters' journey. Our party ideas were pretty rubbish. After three hours, Stan had written down "snacks", "games" and "decorations", while I'd simply doodled page after page of hamsters. It's fair to say I was a little distracted. The one thing we had actually agreed on was that we could use the party organization as cover to retrieve Space Capsule 2. It wasn't much, but it was a start.

As we waited for Stan's dad to pick him up, my dad rushed into the house, his hair looking even more wild.

"I think I've worked it out!" He did a little dance. Boy, he really loved science! "We are so lucky. There will be a short window coming up soon when we can send the hamsters off. If we don't catch that, I estimate it will be roughly three years before the opportunity comes around again."

Three years? That was longer than

most hamsters' lifespans. We *had* to catch the short window.

"So, when is it, Mr Brown?"

"This Friday evening – at precisely seven forty-nine p.m."

Oh bum. That was precisely smack-bang in the middle of the Leavers' Party.

Beep

Beep

Beep

Beep

Beep

Beep ...

CHAPTER TWENTY-ONE

It was all too stressful. When I should have been thinking about the party, I was thinking about the hamsters, and when I was supposed to be thinking about the hamsters, I'd be thinking about the party. With only two days to deal with both, I was not doing a good job of either.

"I just don't see how I can throw the party *and* help Dad send the hamsters off to space," I said despairingly.

Stan rubbed his temples and muttered "Think, think, think" under his breath, which was quite annoying, but I knew he meant well.

"How about…?"

"What if…?"

"Maybe we could…?"

Between us, we'd started many sentences with the hope of them leading to good ideas but every sentence had petered out. I ended up confessing to Stan how I had failed to help Hugh with party planning because the only ideas I'd had were based around hamsters.

Stan suddenly jumped up. "That's it! What if we don't do them separately? What if we combine the two?"

"Do you mean send the hamsters into space AT SCHOOL, *during* the party?"

It was a ridiculous idea. Trying to send hundreds of hamsters into space while holding a party was asking for trouble. But Stan was in full swing.

"Your ideas for the party were perfect. We're *Hamster* Class. Why don't we theme the party around hamsters? We can do, I don't know, hamster-themed crafts and put out hamster snacks and..."

"Sharon could be guest of honour!" I added, suddenly seeing how this idea could *actually* work. "There are games like 'pin the tail on the hamster' and, erm..."

"While all the partying is going on, no one will notice your dad preparing the space capsule out in the playground!"

"We can end with fireworks – so the capsule can be launched unnoticed!"

It was an ambitious plan, but at least it was a plan! And our new name for the Leavers' Party? Well, it just had to be THE HAMSTER BALL!

Ideas for the party started to come thick and fast. Not only would there be fireworks, but Stan came up with zorbing – so pupils could run up and down the school corridors in the human equivalent of a hamster ball. I was going to create a cloak, with all the crocheted hamsters pinned to it – and Stan was going to wear it as Master of Ceremonies. (Miss Harper had told us someone needed to be "Master of Ceremonies", which apparently meant the person who announced what was going on – *definitely* not me.) By the next day, we even had hamster-shaped invitations to send out to our classmates. I was starting to believe that the party could be a success. To keep Stan happy, I even sent an invitation to Hugh.

To

Hamster Class

Please attend our

Spectacular Leavers' Party
The Hamster Ball

Friday, 21st July 6–8 p.m.

Hi Hugh,
I hope you'll come. Everyone wants to see you
and it'd be a shame if you missed it.
I'm sorry we never got on and I'm sorry I said your
name wrong all those years ago. It was a mistake,
but I guess I never properly apologized for it.
I hope your dad's shop is OK
after the pest control scare.
Sorry about that too.
Olly

Through all the party preparations, Dad had been fantastic. He had happily re-jigged some of his calculations so that we could launch the hamsters from school, rather than from our house.

"Seven fifty-five p.m. That's the new time we're aiming for," he announced, which was perfect – right at the end of the party.

Not only was Dad completely calm about preparing the capsule for space, he was also remarkably chilled about the hamsters hanging out in our garden, rebuilding their tunnels under Martha's sandpit. Occasionally, he would weigh and measure a few of them, working out the necessary adjustments for the capsule. I'd barely had time for the hamsters. I missed Tibbles particularly, but he was peeved that I hadn't been letting him come to school. He was pining for Sharon, but I couldn't risk a space hamster being discovered when we were so close to getting them back to their colony. Thankfully, Martha was actually being quite useful for once and played in her sandpit each evening with the hamsters sand-swimming around her.

Dad had even smoothed all the plans over with school. Well, of course, he did *slightly* insist on using the situation as a learning experience for me, so I had to explain our party plans to the Head with Dad by my side. But when Mrs Scout started bringing up concerns about the dangers of fireworks or the risks involved in allowing eleven-year-olds to zorb around school, Dad calmly produced risk assessments he had completed earlier. He also explained that he wanted to take back his Space Capsule 2. ("After thirty years, isn't it time to celebrate some other pupil's work, Mrs Scout?") And Dad said he would replace the space capsule with a mirrored disco ball, which would help everyone get in the party mood, so that was that. Everything was set to make sure that the Leavers' Party would go off with a bang!

Beep

Beep

Beep

Beep

Beep...

CHAPTER TWENTY-TWO

When Friday arrived I was feeling positive – confident, even. OK, so I had failed to complete my poor crocheted hamster, but I chose not to see it as any kind of sign. The other crocheted hamsters were pinned to a long, velvety-brown cloak from the school drama cupboard. Before our classmates headed home to get ready, Stan gave them a twirl. It looked magnificent, skimming his ankles and flying out wide.

After school finished, there was so much for me and Stan to do. In the hall, where the party was to take place, we put out tasty hamster-themed snacks of berries, cucumber, carrots, apple and breadsticks. We prepared tables for craft activities, including making hamsters out of toilet rolls, Hama beads, origami and pom-poms. I was especially pleased with my design for hamster wheels made of paper plates. We had a table for hamster face-painting, although perhaps we should have thought through who was actually going to do the painting! We set up games of "pin the tail on the hamster" and "throw the beanbags into the hamster cheeks", not to mention the "how many hamster poos in the jar?" challenge. The three zorb balls were waiting, temptingly, in the school foyer, but we didn't have time to test them out. And, finally, on the stage, in pride of place, was our guest of honour – Sharon – who was, predictably, asleep.

While we prepped the hall, Dad was outside in the playground, behind a "Danger! Stay Back!" sign, setting up the fireworks and, secretly, the space capsule. The space hamsters were zipped into a large bag with air holes that was hidden in our classroom, waiting for the last moment to get them to the capsule. I had explained the plan in writing to Tibbles that morning, who quietly nodded and accepted the instructions.

As the start time of the party approached, all that was left to do was hang the mirrored disco ball. Stan stood to one side, holding it, while I held the ladder steady for Dad to climb up. Just then, the hall doors opened and in walked Hugh. He looked around.

"I like what you've done," he said. "Hamster theme. Good idea. I guess you guys really did embrace your 'Masters of the Hamsterverse' idea."

This was definitely the nicest thing he'd ever said to me, and I wondered if all I'd needed to do to be his friend had been to apologize. You live and learn.

"I'm glad you came," I responded, surprised to find I actually meant it. "We couldn't have our Year 6 party without you. Do you want to help?"

"Actually, I've brought some snacks,

if that's OK." Hugh nipped out quickly, returning with boxes of goodies from Botham Buys Best. This was probably for the best. Although our hamster snacks looked wholesome and healthy, nothing says "party" more than crisps and chocolate! Hugh smiled. "No nuts – guaranteed!"

As Hugh laid out his snacks, Stan, Dad and I continued trying to hang the disco ball. I had just asked Stan to pass it to me when…

"Oi! Stanley Crump!"

Standing in the door was Amelia Fletcher, all dressed up for the party in something blue and sparkly, but wearing a face of thunder.

"I take it YOU left this … this ABOMINATION by my locker," she shouted, holding up something red in her fingers. "I hate it, and I hate you!"

With that, she threw the fist-sized thing

at Stan before flouncing back out the door. Stan went to catch it – and dropped the disco ball, which smashed, sending hundreds of broken bits of mirror skittering across the floor.

I looked over at what Amelia had thrown. There, on the hall floor, surrounded by shards of mirror that glistened like jewels, was what looked like a heart. Not a love heart but an actual anatomically correct heart with valves and everything, perfectly constructed in crochet. So *that's* what Stan had been making. I felt a pang of guilt. Had I actually spoken to Stan properly about his crush on Amelia, he might have told me what he was doing, and I'd like to think I would have advised him that leaving a bloody-looking crocheted heart in someone's locker was probably not the message he thought it was. Poor Stan.

"My heart! It is shattered like the disco ball!" Stan exclaimed, dramatically clutching his chest. I was about to say something reassuring about Amelia when Stan spoke again. "And look what I've done. There are *hundreds* of mirrors. Each broken mirror is seven years of bad luck – that's seven, fourteen, twenty-one, twenty-eight, thirty-five, forty-one, forty-eight. No. That's not right." Stan started again, counting up in sevens as he pointed to the broken mirror on the floor. The seven times table is the worst.

I led Stan to the side of the hall, wincing as my shoes crunched over the mirror shards, and sat him down on a long wooden bench as he continued to mutter.

I gave up on my friend, located the big, hinged sweeping brush the dinner ladies use at the end of lunch and started pushing it along the floor.

"Let me do that," said Hugh, taking it off me.

"Thank you," I said genuinely.

As Hugh started to clear the floor for me, I finally realized something: Hugh wasn't popular because he bribed his friends with sweets. He was popular because he was *actually* kind.

I surveyed the hall and sighed. Stan was lost in his own seven times table hell, mirror covered the floor, and everyone was supposed to arrive at any moment. I stuck my fingers into my hair and tugged, not sure I could cope with the party if this was how it was going. Not just the party but getting the hamsters safely back to space. Dad climbed down the ladder and gave me a quick hug.

"Surely nothing else can go wrong now," he said, trying to sound reassuring, but which, a few seconds later, was proved entirely incorrect. The hall doors swung open again and standing there, definitely not in a party frock, was Gerald from Black Cat Pest Services.

"I need this place empty. I never found the source of the infestation I was called here to clear and now I'm back to finish the job," announced Gerald, holding his cat in his arms like some kind of movie villain.

That was it. Everything was going horribly wrong. I made a noise that sounded like an injured donkey (probably) and tried to blink away the tears that were forming rapidly in my eyes.

Thankfully, Dad came to the rescue.

"Look," he said, stepping towards Gerald. "The party is about to start and there's dangerous pieces of glass to sweep up. Can't you come back tomorrow, once the kids have enjoyed their party?"

The exterminator did not look convinced. "Something strange is going on here. I can *smell* it. Infestations don't wait for convenient times, you know," said Gerald. "While I'm here, I might as well do some poking around."

Trying any harder to stop him would have aroused more suspicion, so there was nothing more Dad could say. Dad gave me a tiny "I tried" shrug as he folded the ladder, put it away and calmly walked out of the hall. I hoped he was going to stand guard around the space capsule. We certainly couldn't have the exterminator sniffing around there. Stan was still focusing solely on trying to count the number of broken pieces of mirror, so he was less than useless. It was entirely down to me to deal with Gerald. The hamsters were counting on me.

"Be my guest," I said to Gerald, somehow finding my voice. "But I really need to get the party started."

As Hugh finished clearing the floor, Gerald let his black cat jump gracefully out of his arms. It made an immediate beeline for the sleeping Sharon. I decided she was safe in her cage and, to be honest, if the cat was distracted by her, it gave me a chance to do something about the hamsters. As I scurried out of the hall, I grabbed a toilet roll and pen from the craft table and scribbled on it on the way to the classroom.

Once there, I unzipped the bag of hamsters and threw the toilet roll inside. I only hoped Tibbles would get to read it before the others chewed it to pieces. It read:

Exterminator here. Hide where you hid before. Wait for my help to get to the capsule.

It was time to open the doors and let everyone in. My classmates all rushed into the hall and gasped at all the hamster-themed activities, although I suspect that most of them were just happy to see Hugh.

"We need our Master of Ceremonies to get the party started properly," Miss Harper said to me. In honour of the party (I hoped) she was wearing a cream cardigan that looked quite tasteful and plain from the front – until she turned around and revealed a large embroidered hamster taking up the whole of the back. Stan was still sitting on the bench, working out how many years of bad luck he was due. He was in no fit state to fill the role. I grabbed the hamster cloak from his shoulders and held it out to Hugh.

"How about *you* welcome everyone? It would have been your job anyway."

Hugh shook his head. "No. This is your party. You need to speak up. You are the Master of the Hamsterverse."

Unfortunately, Hugh was more right than he knew. So, with that, I was forced into the uncomfortable, stomach-churning position of speaking in public. I pulled the cloak on and walked up the steps at the side of the stage, tripping slightly over the cloak as I moved – it fit Stan much better. The cloak dragged on the floor, and I must have looked like I was being overrun with hamsters.

I stood on the stage, staring out at my

classmates and all the school's teachers, who had clearly already been celebrating the end of the year in the staff room. They stared back at me. Someone coughed. This was horrible. I urged myself to say something – anything!

"Erm."

What a start!

"Errr."

I stood up straight and tried again.

"Hello. Thanks for coming." It wasn't great, but at least I had finally said something. I relaxed a bit and tried to think what Stan would say (when he wasn't busy panicking about broken mirrors or dealing with a broken heart). "Welcome to the Hamster Ball! We have a full hamster-themed party for our farewell to the hamsters. Um, I mean to Hamster Class. Erm. Enjoy yourselves and…"

There was something I was forgetting.

"Oh yes! Make sure you listen out for the instruction to get to the playground at the end of the party for the fireworks."

***

The party was a great success. Everyone loved the crafts and games and soon my classmates were coming up to me and saying how much they were enjoying themselves. Occasionally, I caught sight of Gerald, snooping around, but the bag in the classroom was empty when I went to look. Gerald had found me in there just after I'd checked. He'd grabbed the bag and looked inside.

"And what, exactly, are those?" he said, pointing to the many hamster poos gathered at the bottom of the bag.

"Oh," I said, trying to sound as casual

as possible. "We had a bit of an accident with the 'guess the number of hamster poos in the jar' challenge. It took me *ages* to recount them. Those are – um – spare ones."

Gerald seemed to accept that, but I knew it wouldn't be long before I had to face the problem of how to get hundreds of hamsters out of the ventilation pipes and to the space capsule without him catching me. Even though I was pleased that everyone was having a great time, I was still feeling massively stressed, especially as I had to keep jumping out of the way of zorbing pupils barrelling down the corridors. I checked on the craft activities and was faced with hundreds of hamsters in various states of completion. To be honest, it looked like a hamster bloodbath. Headless pom-pom hamsters lay alongside unwrapped, deformed toilet roll ones. Someone in the blindfold spiked me as they attempted, unsuccessfully, to pin the tail on the hamster, and a stray beanbag flopped on to the side of my head. People kept stepping on the edge of the hamster cloak as it trailed around me.

Without me even noticing, an hour and a half had flown by – and there were only twenty-five minutes left until blast off. Unless I could get the hamsters from the pipes to the space capsule, all of this would have been for nothing.

I went to check on Stan. He'd finally stopped counting the bits of broken mirror and was staring blankly into space.

"How bad is it?"

"About two thousand years, give or take," he said with a sigh. "I guess my bad luck has already started with Amelia hating my gift."

I was about to point out that that had

happened *before* the disco ball smashed, when Seren Simons walked over.

"I saw what you made for Amelia," she said to Stan. "It was good, but I think the right ventricle was a bit too small, and you probably needed some darker red wool to show the veins around the heart if you wanted it to look really realistic."

Seren walked off, but Stan was smiling. I think he felt his luck might have already changed. He turned and looked me up and down.

"You look really silly in that cloak. Glad I'm not the one wearing it. Although at least it fit me. *You* could smuggle an army around under that!"

And with that, not only was Stan back, he had also given me my hamster solution. All I needed to do was take the hamsters, several at a time, outside to Dad, under the safety of the hamster cloak. Perfect.

"But I'm not sure what to do about Gerald and his blasted cat," I said.

"Don't worry. I have a plan for that," said Stan.

While everyone partied, Stan sneakily opened Sharon's cage door, took hold of the sleeping hamster and placed her in his pocket, winking at me. He went up to Miss Harper.

"Miss! Miss! I'm worried about Sharon. Someone's opened her cage and she's no longer in it. What if that cat eats her?"

It did the job and, next thing we knew, Miss Harper was asking Gerald and his cat to leave. Finally, I was able to put my plan into place.

It worked perfectly! I'd spent the entire party milling around, so no one noticed that I was now heading from inside to outside, repeatedly, taking several tens of hamsters at a time, under the safety of the cloak. Even if the odd hamster didn't quite follow my path, the overall effect was just very ... hamstery.

With eight minutes to go until seven fifty-five p.m. – AKA launch time – I had taken all the hamsters to the capsule except one: Tibbles. I knew he'd never forgive me if he didn't have a final chance to say goodbye to Sharon. Tibbles scurried under my cloak as I located Stan, who was happily having his face painted by Seren. He looked nothing like a hamster!

"Stan! Give me Sharon – quick!" I said, trying not to laugh at his smudgy golden face.

Stan patted down his pockets and grimaced.

"She's gone! For real this time!"

Beep

Beep

Beep

CHAPTER TWENTY-THREE

Time was ticking away and there was no sign of Sharon. Tibbles would have to leave Earth without saying goodbye. My last hope was that, by getting everyone into the playground, it would be easier to spot Sharon. Stan agreed to search while I led the party outside. I went up on the stage again.

"Erm!" I wish I could stop starting my announcements like that, but at least I was feeling a bit less terrified than last time. "Hi, everyone. Can you please follow me into the playground?"

Still wearing my cloak, with Tibbles hidden underneath it, I strode through the crowd and, one by one, my classmates started to follow me. I was like a hamster-themed Pied Piper!

Just as I swung open the hall doors, something almost bashed into my face. Thinking it was a zorb ball shooting past, I took a quick step back, but then saw something very strange. And this was strange even for someone secretly helping a colony of space hamsters into a thirty-year-old space capsule while wearing a cloak of crocheted hamsters at a hamster-themed party. In the hallway, there was a bizarre, floating thing which looked like a hamster wheel combined with a jet ski. In it, I could see a hamster. It reminded me of something

I'd seen in *Star Wars*, although I was fairly certain those had been bigger. And not piloted by a hamster. It whirred and buzzed around my head before settling at eye level.

The hamster started chattering and then I noticed that, like Tibbles and Honey Cheeks, this hamster, too, was wearing a black box. The hamster, more unusually,

WE FINALLY MEET!

was wearing what looked like a shiny, ruby-red ring on its head.

"O, so-called God of Hamsters! We finally meet." the black box translated.

"What's going on?" I heard someone ask from the back of the crowd behind me.

"I think it's some kind of entertainment," offered someone else.

"Silence!" commanded the hamster.

The hamster jabbed at various buttons in front of him, and I noticed that his console appeared to be formed out of an old calculator. Could that be Dad's old scientific calculator? Surely this was Fluffy the 1000th! How on earth had the evil hamster survived the collision with the spaceship?

"Fluffy the 1000th, I take it?" I said, trying to sound fearsome and god-like but, rather, sounding a bit pant-wetty.

"Fluffy the 1000th, the Great and

Most Fluffisome, Tender-Hearted Leader of Hamsters," corrected Fluffy the 1000th (the Great and Most Fluffisome, Tender-Hearted Leader of Hamsters). "You have somehow survived, nay thwarted, my plans. And now here we are. You, with nowhere to escape, and me, with this weapon trained on you."

The crowd behind me gasped as Fluffy pointed to the front of his floating vehicle. What looked like the barrel of a gun – or some kind of shooting device – appeared.

"Before I kill you, I would like to see the traitor Tibbles, who failed so abysmally at his mission to destroy you and your planet."

"It's very tense," I heard Miss Harper say. "I had no idea Olly Brown was interested in acting."

"I wish they'd done this show on the stage so we could all see properly," someone else complained. "And the special effects are rubbish. Is that a Fruit Polo on that mouse's head?"

I tried to block out the crowd.

"Tibbles didn't fail. He had his faith and he found what he was looking for. He didn't know he was being set up by you. I will *never* let you have him."

"You tell 'im, Olly!" cried one of my classmates.

"Boo! Down with Fluffy the 1000th!" yelled another.

"So be it!" said Fluffy, and he swung his small ship further out into the corridor to get a better aim.

At that moment, Tibbles appeared from under my cloak.

"What's happening now? I can't see!" Amelia whinged.

Fluffy the 1000th squeaked at Tibbles and the black box translated.

"Tibbles! You are a disgrace to our colony. You valued your faith over submitting to my *tender-hearted* leadership. I will destroy you here, in front of your god, as a lesson to all others."

Tibbles sat upright and faced Fluffy the 1000th without flinching. The weapon barrel started to glow red.

Just at that moment, a chirping resonated along the corridor and a zorb ball suddenly careered towards us. I stepped

backwards out of its path and Fluffy the 1000th had to swoop up to avoid being taken out. As it passed before my eyes, there, running like I'd never seen her run before, was Sharon! Somehow, she had timed her pass not only to disturb Fluffy the 1000th's aim, but also to use the zorb to pick up Tibbles. Sharon! I gawped after the translucent orb as it disappeared around the corner, a small, sleek, golden hamster and a large, tufty white-and-brown one running inside it, their legs a blur.

It took Fluffy the 1000th a moment to gather himself and I stepped back inside the hall, letting the doors close in front of my face.

"WOW!" cried Hugh, next to me. "What happens now?"

Sadly, what happened was that Fluffy the 1000th pushed through the hall doors, and I cursed myself for not somehow locking the door or blocking his path. The crowd backed away behind me.

"So, the traitor Tibbles has escaped," Fluffy the 1000th continued. "But no mind. I have all the time in the world to find and destroy that hamster – just after I destr—"

But Fluffy the 1000th got no further.

The hall doors crashed open again and a man with a bald head, a neon T-shirt and a beeping hand-held device leapt in. Mr Potter! I'd completely forgotten about him.

"There it is!" he screamed. "Catch it."

The next part all happened very quickly.

Ten people, all dressed the same in dark, military-looking uniforms, with tinted goggles, wearing black knitted hats rushed into the hall. If you looked closely enough, the name GAIL was embroidered in dark thread on their jackets. Between them, they threw a kind of bag over Fluffy the 1000th and his floating hamster-wheel vehicle.

"We've done it! I was right!" yelled Mr Potter, his face turning bright red with glory. "The name Harold Potter will go down in history as the first person to track an alien species!"

Two of the GAIL people grabbed Mr Potter under his arms and dragged him back through the hall door, as the others wrestled Fluffy the 1000th away. The final GAIL person paused briefly and stared around the room.

"You never saw this and this never happened!"

The doors swung closed behind them.

Silence. Except for rustling sounds from the teachers, who had been distracted by the sight of the child-free snack table and taken the opportunity to stuff their faces. Their cheeks bulged like – well, you know.

My class stood in shock for a few seconds more – and then … the hall erupted in whooping and cheering! Everyone loves drama.

I could feel myself sweating under my hamster cloak, and would have quite liked a moment to catch my breath and/or have a minor heart attack – but looking at my watch told me we had ninety seconds left before blast off!

"Follow me!" I shouted, and everyone ran out into the playground.

We all gathered at a safe distance from the fireworks and I was about to run to Dad when Stan caught me and thrust something into my hands. It was a black box! It must have been the one Fluffy the 1000th had been wearing, knocked off by the people in black.

Dad was watching the countdown

click down when I reached him. Forty-five seconds to go.

"You'd better get back," he said. "I need to start lighting these fireworks if we're going to hide the space capsule's path."

"Has Tibbles made it out here?" I asked.

Dad shook his head.

Thirty seconds to go. It was too late to do anything. I ran back to Stan.

Fireworks started shooting across the sky.

"Is Tibbles on board?" asked Stan.

I had a lump in my throat and couldn't speak. Any second now, the faithful space hamsters would leave my life for ever – but they were missing their leader.

Stan jabbed a finger in my side and said, "Look!"

Only just visible in the glow of the fireworks was a tiny, golden hamster racing across the playground towards the space capsule. He was going to make it!

Another thought struck me. *I* hadn't said goodbye. I'd ferried every hamster to safety and said farewell to each of them – but my goodbye to Tibbles had been cruelly cut short by Fluffy the 1000th.

I counted down, under my breath, to the time of the space capsule's launch. To everyone else, it would probably look like a big, bright firework – one that just kept going and going – but I knew what it was and tears started falling down my cheeks.

"The end of primary school is a big thing," said Miss Harper, who was suddenly standing next to me. "Just see what you've achieved here. You have definitely made an impact. Target three – tick!"

That wasn't why I was crying, of course, but I appreciated it anyway.

"Do you think you might be able to look after Sharon for the holidays?" she continued. "As the class hamster monitor, it seems only right."

**

The end of the party was very strange. Everyone from Hamster Class congratulated me and Stan for an awesome night, but I felt as empty and deflated as the two remaining zorb balls, now limply strewn over some hall chairs. The third zorb ball was still missing. As each class member left, in what felt like a bizarre ceremony, they unpinned their own crocheted hamster from my cloak to take home. Finally, after Stan had unpinned all eight of his, he handed one to me.

"There you go, mate. Have one of mine," he said.

I handed it back to him. "I'm OK, thanks. I don't think crocheted hamsters will ever be my thing."

Dad appeared from outside, flushed with success.

"Did you see? It went up beautifully!" he said, beaming. "I'm heading into the office to track it on our systems – and then, of course, delete all evidence of it!"

I smiled sadly at Dad. "Thanks, Dad. And at least Tibbles made it in time."

Dad looked confused.

"No. Yes. I mean no," he said. "Yes, he appeared at the capsule and he chattered to the hamsters, but then he ran off. I guess he was saying goodbye. He must be around here somewhere."

"You mean Tibbles didn't leave?" I cried.

I sprinted along the corridor, thrusting

my hand in my pocket to retrieve the little black box Stan had given me.

"Tibbles!" I shouted. "Tibbles!"

Each time I called, the black box squeaked away in my hand.

Finally, past all the turns of the school corridor, by the fire escape, I found the missing zorb ball. I was excited to speak to Tibbles properly for the first time and, as I approached the zorb, I could hear chattering and chirping. The black box translated.

"Let me feed you another blueberry, my gloriously huge, hairy goddess..."

I paused, smiled, then turned and walked back up the corridor.

On second thoughts, I had plenty of time to catch up with Tibbles later. He wasn't going anywhere. Not only that, I had an entire summer of Sharon to look forward to, and, by the sounds of it, quite possibly a whole new colony of space–Earth hamsters to deal with soon too. Hopefully, though, this time, I could just be Olly Brown, *Friend* of Hamsters!

TOP SECRET

After all the excitement of capturing our first ever intergalactic life-form, I am disappointed to report our initial tests are telling us the specimen is nothing more than a hamster, scientific name cricetinae.

Based on the superior technology we retrieved during our mission, however, there is certainly something strange about this situation. The specimen also appears to be attempting to communicate with us. We must undertake further tests to see whether the specimen could *actually* be a shape-shifting alien species that has taken on the form of one of Earth's most common pets. It would be the perfect cover. Dave is preparing the deep-probe now.

This information is highly sensitive

and confidential. Our discovery must remain secret. For this reason, we have removed all details of the person who alerted us to the specimen's presence. We have wiped his memory and given him a new name. No one can ever know the name of Mr Harold Potter.

ACKNOWLEDGEMENTS

Thank you so much to Scholastic and the whole team there for your continued support. My editor, Linas Alsenas, is simply brilliant and I love any opportunity to work with him because he always makes my ideas better! There are many other people who worked behind the scenes to get this book finished, from the copyeditor to the designer to the publicity department. A massive thank you goes to: Sarah Dutton, Sarah Baldwin, Jessica White, Harriet Dunlea and Stephanie Lee.

I'm delighted to work with Jack Noel, whose wonderful illustrations really help bring my stories to life. One day, we might even meet in person! And thank you to Jo Williamson, my ace agent extraordinaire.

Writing can be a rather solitary job so I'm lucky to have a growing group of writer friends, who offer support and encouragement – you know who you are! I'm also thrilled to be getting to know wonderful booksellers and glorious independent bookshops. Special mentions go to the Rabbit Hole Bookshop in Brigg, Wonderland Bookshop in Retford and Drake the Bookshop in Stockton – encouraging reading and a love of books in areas that didn't traditionally have bookshops is a fabulous thing and, quite simply, helps the life chances of all children you are able to reach. Thank you.

And, finally, thank you to my friends and family for everything. A huge (not Hugh) thanks goes to Helen Genney, my super-talented teacher friend who inspired me with her crocheting abilities and even helped me create my own crocheted hamster (which will be accompanying me on school visits). Particular thanks goes to my impressive and intrepid mother-in-law, Jo, who has made it possible for me to attend events and author visits, and many other things besides. Thanks to my children for being lovely enough for my mother-in-law to look after without too many problems. And thank you to Robin, my rock.

BETHANY WALKER

writes funny books for children.
Before she became an author,
she was a teacher and then an
educator in museums and galleries.
She has two children and
lives in Lincolnshire.

JACK NOEL

is an author, illustrator and
designer of children's books.
Originally from Brighton, today
he lives in London with his
wife and two children.

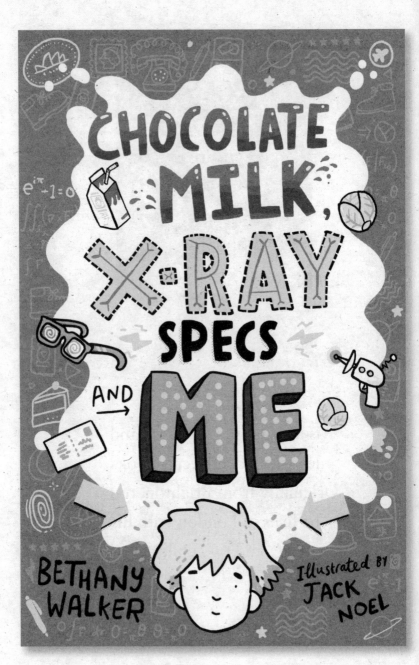

CHOCOLATE MILK, X-RAY SPECS AND ME

BETHANY WALKER

Illustrated BY JACK NOEL

I SPY ...
A TOTALLY CLUELESS BOY!

Freddy is looking forward to his upcoming birthday party, so he writes and posts actual letters (on paper!) to his parents, who he believes are working at a Brussels-sprouts farm in Outer Castonga, with no internet or phone access.

But the truth is, Freddy's parents are secret agents out of the country on a highly classified mission – and Freddy has NO IDEA! His parents have hidden secret missile codes somewhere in the house, and bad guys have arrived to try to find them – in terrible disguises. But no disguise is too terrible for Freddy, no clue too obvious!

Will he *ever* catch on?

A HILARIOUS ART HEIST MYSTERY THAT WILL STEAL YOUR HEART!

The country is gripped with Mona Lisa Fever! The Royal Family has announced a huge reward for the return of a missing version of the *Mona Lisa*, stolen from their palace over 200 years ago.

But in the town of Colpepper, Mia has a different art problem: she loves art, but her underfunded school is closing down the art department! But there's more to her school than meets the eye. Little-known local legend has it that the historic building contains a hidden vault, perhaps containing the *Lost Mona Lisa*! So Mia has no idea that scheming criminals are hiding among the school staff.

Can Mia solve the mystery of the Mona Lisa before it's too late?